# DRAGON ORB

## Shadow

# MARK ROBSON

**SIMON AND SCHUSTER**

SIMON AND SCHUSTER

First published in Great Britain by Simon and Schuster UK Ltd, 2009
A CBS COMPANY

1 3 5 7 9 10 8 6 4 2

Simon & Schuster UK Ltd
1st Floor
222 Gray's Inn Road
London WC1X 8HB

A CIP catalogue record for this book is
available from the British Library

ISBN 978-1-84738-069-2

Typeset by Rowland Phototypesetting Ltd,
Bury St Edmunds, Suffolk
Printed and bound in Great Britain by
CPI Cox & Wyman Ltd, Reading, Berkshire

For Anne McCaffrey

It is impossible for me to write a series like
this without paying tribute to 'The Grand
Dragonlady of Pern'. I always said I would
never write dragon stories because, for me,
Anne owned dragons. In the end
I just could not resist!

This dedication comes with gratitude for
all the wonderful stories that entertained
me in my teenage years . . . and in all
the years since!

# Acknowledgements

A huge thank you to my editor, Heather, for her encouragement, her hard work and her patience!

Many thanks also to my team of proof readers, but in particular to: Diane, Patrick and my 'Mary Godmother', whose help, support and 'eagle eyes' have been invaluable.

*Also by Mark Robson*

Dragon Orb 1: Firestorm

Imperial Spy
Imperial Assassin
Imperial Traitor

For information on future
books and other stories
by Mark Robson, visit:
www.markrobsonauthor.com

# Contents

## Chapter One
# 'Imagine You're a Bird.'

*Release the dark orb – death brings me life.*
*Take brave ones' counsel, 'ware ye the knife.*
*Exercise caution, stay pure and heed,*
*Yield unto justice: truth will succeed.*

'They should've listened to me,' Pell muttered as he powered away from the campsite on Shadow's back. 'Kira can twist my words all she likes, but I should be the leader of this quest.'

As he considered his three companions, it took a moment for Pell to realise he was grinding his teeth in frustration. In his heart he felt the Oracle's Great Quest to seek out the fabled dragon orbs and return them to the Dragon Spirit in the heart of Orupee's highest mountain range was a task worthy of heroes. Why then had the Oracle chosen these others to go with him? Kira, rider of the dusk dragon, Longfang, was perhaps the most irritating. Of the three she showed the most promise, but she was stubborn and would not listen to reason.

'*Don't fret, dragonrider,*' his night dragon, Shadow, whispered in his mind, her silky voice caressing. '*They'll see things differently when we return with the night orb.*'

Pell had always marvelled at Shadow's voice, so totally at odds with her fearsome exterior. If he closed his eyes and listened to that voice in his head, it was easy to imagine Shadow as a beautiful maiden, dark and mysterious. And she *was* beautiful – it just took a certain perspective to see past the vicious horns and teeth of the enormous night dragon.

'*They need our strength,*' Shadow continued. '*Firestorm and Nolita are hopeless. I've never seen such an unlikely partner for a day dragon. Given their weaknesses, it is hard to see why the others want to seek the day orb first.*'

Shadow was right. How Elian, rider of a dawn dragon, could describe Nolita as 'brave' was beyond him. The boy was so naïve! The blond girl was the most craven person Pell had ever met. Nolita was pretty enough, with her delicate features and her fine blond hair, but her cringing and weeping was repulsive. Kira, on the other hand, was annoying –

but at least there was some fire in her personality. The Racafian tribal girl went out of her way to appear fierce, with her face paint and her weapons. Given the right set of circumstances, Pell would have found her interesting. In reality, however, he knew they would likely clash over most issues.

'I'm better off working alone,' he breathed.

'*You'll never be alone,*' Shadow purred in his mind.

'Of course not, Shadow,' he replied, quickly. 'Sorry. I phrased that badly. I didn't mean to exclude you. I should have said, "We're better off working independently." We make a fantastic team, you and I, and we're destined for greatness. Why else were we chosen for the Great Quest? There won't be any dull peace talks or boring guard duties in our future. We'll do deeds that will be the talk of generations.'

The soothing rhythm of Shadow's wingbeats and the exhilaration he felt as they climbed between the mountains calmed Pell's thoughts. Higher and higher they went, until even the highest peaks fell away beneath them. Looking down from such a lofty height, it was easy to imagine himself as king of the world. How could anyone in Areth who did not ride a dragon believe they were lord over anything? To soar above the highest mountains was an experience reserved for the elite. No walls were high enough to deny him entry. The world was his playground. Who would argue with the rider of a dragon like Shadow? None but a fool – a fool with a death wish.

The Oracle's riddling words might be twisted beyond comprehension, but Pell could see the path they paved in his mind's eye. It glittered as if studded with diamonds. Glory awaited him. He could feel it in his heart as surely as the sun would set.

Silently he urged Shadow on. For two season rotations he had longed for the acceptance and respect of his fellow night dragon riders. Until now, they had treated him as a boy, because he had not yet visited the Oracle. This time it would be different, he thought, satisfaction warming his stomach with a burning sensation that was pure pleasure. His was a special destiny – the night dragon rider entrusted with the fate of the Oracle. By his actions the Dragon Spirit would live or die. It was an awesome responsibility and one with which he would prove his worth.

The air was bitterly cold as they cruised across the mountain range. While the wind at ground level had dropped to nothing, here, thousands of spans up into the sky, a steady westerly breeze aided their journey. Pell let go of the pommel and clapped his mitts together a few times in an effort to trigger more blood flow. His fingers, toes, cheeks, ears and the tip of his nose were numb, but he was reluctant to ask Shadow to descend. He was eager to cover as much ground as possible before they took a break. It took a lot of effort and energy for Shadow to get up this high, so they should make the most of it.

The sun marched steadily across the sky as they pressed eastwards, but although it blazed golden in the clear blue heavens, Pell felt none of its warmth. By the time the final majestic peaks slipped past slowly beneath them, he knew he had to descend, or risk frostbite. He had seen other riders with missing fingers and toes. The cold was a subtle and sadistic enemy.

'*Let's go down, Shadow,*' he projected. He doubted that his lips could form the words even if he wished to speak aloud. '*I need to warm up and I'm sure you would welcome a short break.*'

'*Your endurance does you credit,*' Shadow replied. '*Not many riders show your resilience. We have already flown far today. With our combined strength we will reach the enclave faster than many would believe possible.*'

Pell wanted to smile at her praise, but the muscles in his face were too cold to respond. He loved it when Shadow talked like this. It made him feel warm inside. He had known from the instant they had met that they were perfectly matched. They were both competitive and strong. They both wanted power and recognition. Perhaps more importantly, however, they both recognised the potential their joining offered. A strong dragon with a strong rider could do great things.

Shadow eased gently into a shallow dive. As they accelerated, the wind-rush began to build and Pell bent low over the pommel of his saddle in an effort to reduce the biting chill of the bitter airflow. In order to crouch so low, he had to lean to one side or the other of the great ridge of dragon horn in front of the saddle. He chose to lean to the left. Initially this was fine, but as their speed continued to increase Pell suddenly realised that the force of the air was dragging him further left and out of the saddle.

He tried to pull himself back up straight, but his body refused to respond. Panic flashed through him. His hands had no strength to grip. His legs were numb with cold against the dragon's back. He could not tell if his feet were still in the stirrups. There was nothing he could do. Without a miracle, he was going to fall.

'*Shadow!*' he called through the bond. He was unsure if he had managed to mouth the name aloud, or if the call was purely mental. '*I'm slipping!*'

'*Try to hold on, Pell. I've never been very good at catching,*' she replied, trying to slow down without making Pell's predicament worse. It was not easy. The slightest force might prove fatal, so her delicate efforts had little immediate effect.

'*I'm too cold,*' he admitted, a growing sense of horror building fast. '*All my strength has gone.*'

It was awful. He had never felt so weak. Hearing Shadow's admission made it worse. If he fell and she could not catch him, he would die. To survive a fall from this height was unthinkable. In the two rotations they had been together he had only felt close to falling once before, and that had been momentary. This was different. He had got himself into this situation through foolishly pushing on in the extreme cold.

His body slid a little further. He tried with all his might to pull himself back up into the saddle, but he had passed the point of no return. Little by little his fingers slipped from their precarious hold on the pommel. He could feel his heart tightening with horror. Suddenly he lost his grip altogether.

'*Pell!*' Shadow's mental voice was full of panic as she felt him slip from the saddle.

A heartbeat later Pell was hanging upside down by his left foot, which was caught in the stirrup. He bounced against Shadow's side, the airflow flinging him around with invisible hands.

'*I'm still with you,*' he replied, grunting as his body thumped repeatedly against the dragon's scales. '*But I'm not sure for how long.*'

He looked up at where his foot was trapped, then down at the long, long drop to the ground, thousands of spans below. His boot was firmly wedged, but the foot inside the boot was not. He had always preferred his boots to be a slightly looser fit than was fashionable. A horrible feeling in the pit of his stomach told him this was a preference he was about to regret.

With gritted teeth he twisted his body and reached up towards the stirrup. Trembling with the effort he forced his mitts closer and closer, but the more he tried to reach towards his trapped foot, the more savagely the wind flailed him against Shadow's side until a particularly violent impact left him seeing stars and forced him to straighten.

Pell was strong. It was one of his defining characteristics. Under any other circumstance he would have grabbed the stirrup with ease, but the cold had robbed him of his flexibility and strength. It was so frustrating he wanted to scream, but he resisted the temptation. Ignoring all sensations of disorientation and discomfort, he tried again.

Fighting the wind and the stiffness in his body with every ounce of muscle power he could muster, he forced his hands up towards the stirrup again. Little by little his hands stretched closer and closer.

'Aaarrrrrghhhh!' The growling roar ripped from his throat as somehow he found the final ounce of strength he needed. His right hand grabbed hold of the stirrup at the precise moment that his foot slipped free of his boot. For a moment he hung there, scrabbling to reach the stirrup with his other hand to strengthen his hold, but his weight and the pull of the wind was too much for his numb fingers. Despite his very best effort, his grip failed and he fell.

'*Shadow!*' His call was instinctive and instant.

'*Pell!*'

Shadow tipped into a steep spiral dive, but held off folding her wings completely until she was positioned perfectly above him.

'*Spread your arms and legs,*' she ordered him. '*Try to imagine you are a bird.*'

'*Imagine I'm a bird? I don't have wings, damn it!*'

'*No,*' Shadow agreed, her mental voice returning to her normal soft tones. '*But if you want me to catch you, then you must calm yourself and do as I say. Try to stabilise your body so that you are falling flat on your stomach, with your arms and legs stretched out. That*

9

*way you will fall more slowly. It will make it easier for me to catch up with you.'*

The calm tones of Shadow's voice in his head were a tonic. The unfamiliar feeling of fear had spiked through Pell's mind and a metallic taste formed at the back of his mouth. The dragon's soft voice of reason, giving him clear directions, helped him regain a measure of control as he struggled to do what she asked of him. Initially he stabilised himself on his back, but with a little experimentation, he managed to flip over onto his stomach and stay flat, with his arms outstretched and his hands cupped. He did not feel as if he was falling any slower. If anything, he felt as if he was falling faster than ever.

*'That's good, Pell. Just hold that position. I'll be with you shortly.'*

He was falling blind. He tried cracking open his eyelids the tiniest sliver to see how far he was from the ground, but it was no use. The wind was too strong. It prevented him from seeing anything. How long had he been falling? It felt like for ever, but that was most likely his imagination. Where was Shadow? Surely if she was going to catch him, she would do it soon?

A sudden swirling bump of air sent him tumbling out of control again. Pell panicked. His heart was

10

thumping so hard in his chest that it felt as if it might burst free.

'*Shadow!*'

'*Sorry about that,*' Shadow said softly in his mind. '*My closure speed was too high. If I'd grabbed you, I might have killed you with the impact. Stay calm. Get back into the position you were in before. I'll try again in a moment.*'

'*We must be running out of height—*'

'*Let me worry about that,*' Shadow said quickly. '*Get back on your stomach. I can't catch you if you keep tumbling.*'

Pell did as he was told. It took a heartbeat or two, but he managed to settle into a face-down position again. How long had he got? He could not get the thought out of his mind. It could not be long now. Was there really time for another attempt? He could feel Shadow's concentration through the bond. She would do everything in her power to save him. The surety in that thought was an incredible source of comfort. Her focus gave him such hope that little by little he began to feel himself relax.

'Oof!'

The talons crashed hard into his back and legs, but he cared nothing for the pain as they closed around him. He was safe, he realised. Shadow had

11

done it. She had caught him. The relief and the pain, combined with the sudden crushing force that took his breath away as they pulled out of their headlong dive, were all too much. In the blink of an eye, Pell spiralled swiftly into the sweet oblivion of unconsciousness.

## Chapter Two
# Very Tasty

'*You're doing really well, Nolita,*' Firestorm the day dragon told her as they flew out from the top of the volcano and turned northwards. '*Try to distract your mind from the things that cause you most distress. You could try counting my wingbeats. The repetition should help calm you.*'

Nolita clung to the suggestion like a lifeline. No sooner had they cleared the volcano's rim than the ground fell away beneath them and her fear of heights loomed over her like a dark wave. It felt as if the crushing weight of it might crash down on her at any moment. Her stomach tightened and her breathing quickened. She had nothing left to throw up, but that would not stop her retching if she could not master the fear.

Counting was a good idea, she realised. She could

even count with her eyes closed, which would save her looking down. Her main worry with this was that the smooth, rhythmic rising and falling of Firestorm's back might send her to sleep. Although it was not yet an hour past midday, she felt exhausted.

Nolita had been the first of the four riders to be tested. Her nervous anticipation of today had kept her awake most of the previous night. The emotional trauma of the test of bravery in the Chamber of the Sun's Steps, together with the pain and shock of the dragon orb sucking blood from her fingers, had left her feeling weak and drained of energy. The experience still felt unreal, like a particularly intense dream. However, she knew that if she reached down into her saddlebag, she would feel the globe that was the day orb. It seemed like a miracle, but somehow she had risen to the challenge. All she had to do was to return the orb to the Oracle and her part of the quest would be over.

'*Thank you, Firestorm. I'll try,*' she replied aloud. '*I'd like to keep my eyes shut as I count, but I'm worried about falling asleep.*'

'*Don't fret, dragonrider. I will warn you if I sense you are sliding towards sleep. And please, call me Fire. Most dragonriders use a shortened form of their dragon's name.*'

Dragonrider. She, Nolita, was a dragonrider! Who would ever have thought it? For as long as she could remember, Nolita had suffered a terrible fear of all large creatures – even the most gentle ones. Add to that a terror of heights that had prevented her from playing even the most simple of climbing games as a child, and the miraculous nature of her current situation became apparent. The idea that she would ever ride high in the sky on a dragon's back was laughable, and yet here she was. If only my brother and my sister could see me now, she thought. They would be amazed.

'*Thank you, Fire. I appreciate your help and understanding,*' she said, realising with a start that she had not answered him. Her thoughts were so easily distracted at the moment. '*I'm not sure this will ever be easy, but I'll try.*'

Closing her eyes, she began. 'One, two, three . . .' By the time she reached thirty, her heart rate began to drop and the tight feeling of sickness in her stomach started to subside. There was still a bitter taste at the back of her mouth, but she ignored it and continued counting.

Kira glanced left at Nolita to see how she was doing. Nolita was flying on Firestorm alongside Kira's dusk dragon, Fang. Elian was riding his dawn

15

dragon, Aurora, ahead of them, leading the way northwards towards Orupee and the Oracle's cave.

At dawn tomorrow, Aurora was planning to make a gateway into the other world. Aurora could have created the gateway at the enclave of the day dragons. There was no limitation on where she created them, but gateways could only be formed at dawn, when the barriers between worlds were at their weakest. Elian had pushed them into beginning the journey immediately after Nolita's triumph at the test of bravery. He had made her face up to her fears and ride her dragon again, cleverly reinforcing the boost in self-confidence she had gained. Nolita could hardly refuse to climb back onto her dragon in front of her entire enclave.

'*Fang?*' Kira asked. '*Do you know where we're going to find the griffins that Barnabas mentioned?*'

Barnabas, senior rider at the day dragon enclave, had identified the 'brave ones' from the Oracle's verse about the second orb as the half-lion, half-eagle creatures of legend. Even the dragons acknowledged the wisdom of the elderly rider, so Kira felt sure his interpretation of the riddling words was right.

'*I have some idea, yes,*' Fang replied with an amused chuckle that rumbled around in her mind.

'*What's so funny? It would be good to have some idea*

of where the next orb might be. So where will we be heading?'

'I'd rather not say just yet. Aurora and I decided it would be better to wait until we had everyone together. It's funny, because we had just decided that you would be the first rider to start thinking about the griffins, when you asked. It must be your hunter's instinct.'

'I'd say it was common sense,' she replied. 'But we need to find Pell first, and that might not be so easy. Let's start with that. Where's the enclave of the night dragons? Have you ever been there?'

Just speaking Pell's name set Kira bristling with barely concealed anger. The boy's arrogance had led him to abandon them before the quest had begun. He had not listened to reason, but instead insisted that the Oracle's reference to the 'brave ones' had meant the leaders of the night dragon enclave. His misinterpretation and pig-headedness had set him on a course that could spell disaster. If the night dragon leader discovered what they were doing, he would move against them. That did not bear thinking about.

'I have seen it from a distance,' Fang said warily. 'The enclave is in the largest of the mountain ranges in Isaa. It's not a good idea to get too close unless you are a night dragon. They are very protective of their enclave. I do not want to sound prejudiced, but the night dragons

17

are not welcoming to other dragon types the way that day, dusk and dawn dragons are.'

'So how are we going to make contact with Pell and Shadow if they have reached the enclave before we get there?' Kira asked.

'Well, the sensible option would be to wait for them to leave,' Fang suggested. 'If they get there before us, then the night dragons will already know that the Great Quest is underway. From what Barnabas said, that will spell trouble. What sort of trouble, I would rather not guess. The night dragons have an unsavoury reputation when it comes to dealing with those who stand in their way.'

'Great!' Kira growled. 'So we get to sit and wait for pretty boy, while he makes life difficult for us.' She fell silent for a moment as she started doing some quick mental calculations. 'Fang, how long will it take Pell to get to the night dragon enclave from the Oracle?'

'Depending on the weather, it takes about a week,' Fang replied thoughtfully. 'But Shadow is a very strong dragon. She might do it faster.'

'A week? Hmm. We've been gone six days from the Oracle. He's probably not there yet. I wonder . . .'

'What do you wonder?' Fang asked, intrigued.

'I wonder if we should go straight to the night dragon enclave rather than the Oracle,' she mused. 'We could intercept Shadow and bring Pell back to the Oracle before going off to find the griffins.'

'That is a good idea,' Fang admitted. 'But we should not make the decision alone. Let's talk to the others about it later. I think the urgency of getting the day orb to the Oracle will probably outweigh the danger posed by Pell's impetuous trip to the night dragon enclave.'

Kira was not convinced, but she could see that Fang was right about discussing it with the others. If they were to change their course, then they should all agree on it. She looked at Elian on Aurora's back and then at Nolita. Did the girl have her eyes closed? It was hard to be certain from this distance, but it did look that way. Kira arched her eyebrows as she considered what it would be like to fly with her eyes closed. She was not sure she would like to do it for more than a few heartbeats. Flying in cloud and heavy rain when it was difficult to see was bad enough, but to fly completely blind – just the thought of it sent a shudder down her spine.

They landed in the late afternoon near a small lake. No sooner had they touched down than Nolita dismounted and made straight for the water's edge to wash. Dipping her hands into the lake she scrubbed and rubbed at her skin with vicious thoroughness. Kira and Elian left her to it.

Having witnessed her bravery in the day dragon

enclave earlier, Nolita's quirky behaviour and strange little rituals now seemed somehow more acceptable. It took a special kind of strength to face one's worst fears and overcome them. Nolita needed the rituals to help her do this. Kira found all the hand-washing a source of irritation, but she could see the positive effect it had on the blond girl. It kept her going. Kira was not foolish enough to interfere with anything that achieved this.

They spoke little as they set up camp. There was no need. Each of them had settled into a routine, so they got on with their tasks and worked until the shelter was complete, a fire set, and an adequate pile of fuel gathered to feed the flames through the night. With all the major tasks complete, they settled around the fire to heat water for drinks and to cook food for their evening meal.

Kira raised the subject of going directly after Pell, but both Elian and Nolita were quick to oppose her.

'What if something goes wrong?' Elian asked. 'What if the night dragons steal the first orb? The quest is on enough of a knife-edge already. Don't complicate it, Kira.'

'The orb must go to the Oracle immediately,' Nolita added firmly, not allowing Kira the opportunity to respond to Elian's questions.

One look at Nolita's expression said it all. Kira let the matter drop. In her heart, however, she felt they might all come to regret this decision. Her instincts were screaming at her that they should go after Pell before it was too late, but she knew that to split the group further would spell the end of the quest. To succeed they needed Aurora's gateways to speed them from place to place. As Aurora was Elian's dragon, he had become the unlikely leader of the group, which grated a little.

Kira glanced at him across the fire. He was lost in thought, staring at the flames. With his fair hair and serious blue eyes, he was a nice enough boy, but he wasn't ready to lead a quest like this. He was too naïve. Yes, he was brave and adventurous, but he had no experience of the world outside of his little village. He did have some useful skills, but he was too quick to defer to others to be an effective leader. He did challenge things if he didn't agree, but he lacked the instincts Kira had gained during her training as a hunter. What was the core of this quest if not a hunt? She was far more suited to be the leader than he was.

The evening was warm, and the fire unnecessary other than for cooking. Though it was supposedly the height of summer, this region saw little seasonal variation in weather. The temperate climate in

21

Orupee was far more variable. What will it be like in Isaa? she wondered. Isaa was on the far side of Areth. She was not even sure whether it was north or south of the equator. Would it be summer or winter there now?

A slight sound set her senses tingling. Something was moving in the grass behind her, closing with the stealth of a predator. Muscles tensed, she slid her hand to the hilt of her belt knife and slowly turned her head. Neither of her compatriots looked up. They were both lost in their own thoughts. It was hard to see anything outside of the cocoon of light that surrounded the fire. Shadows danced in sympathy with the flames, but there were no telltale reflections from hunting eyes that she could see.

For a moment, Kira began to wonder if she were imagining it. The edge of the lake was only a handful of paces away. How could anything hide in such a small area? A slight movement in her peripheral vision set her heart racing again. It was a snake – a huge snake.

'Gods!' she breathed. She had seen a lot of snakes during her hunting trips, but nothing like this one. Its undulating body was far thicker than her thigh and it was so long that the middle of its body was still emerging from the water. She froze. Movement would attract its attention. It was far less likely to attack if it did not perceive her as a threat. What was it doing this close to a fire? Snakes were normally shy creatures.

The others were still not aware of it, but Kira was hesitant to speak. Any noise might trigger an attack.

'Fang?' she asked silently.

'I see it, Kira. Stay still.'

'Where are you?'

'Not far. I've camouflaged, but as soon as I move it will feel me coming. Its whole body is sensitive to movement and I won't be able to mask my approach. I don't want to trigger it to attack before I can intervene. The orb is drawing it.'

'The orb? How?'

'It's giving off such a strong scent of blood that it's probably attracting every predator for leagues around,' Fang replied, his voice sounding casual.

'A little warning would have been nice. How long have you known?' Kira asked, watching with a growing sense of horror as the snake gathered its coils.

'Ever since we landed,' Fang admitted. 'Dragons are not as sensitive to blood as some predators, but we all noticed it. We didn't want to worry you unnecessarily. I'd say this further strengthens the argument for taking it to the Oracle and ridding ourselves of it as soon as possible.'

The snake's mouth began to open and Kira could

no longer control the urge to draw her knife. The steel blade flashed in the light of the fire as she whipped it from her belt. She drew her weapon and the great head lashed forwards towards her, jaws gaping. She flinched, slashing the air with the blade, body braced against the expected impact of the huge reptile. To her surprise the strike did not reach her, for as the snake lunged so Longfang's invisible jaws bit into its mid-section.

Nolita's hands rose instinctively to her cheeks and she screamed, the sound reverberating across the water as vast coils of the snake whipped up into the air, wrapping around Fang's neck and rapidly constricting in an attempt to crush the dragon's throat. Elian was on his feet and shouting. Kira scrambled around the fire to join them. Huddling behind the tiny tongues of flame, they used the fire as a fragile shield whilst they watched in fascinated horror as the two giant reptiles twisted, locked in combat. The dragon's cloak of camouflage disappeared as the huge weight of the snake dragged him down.

'*Fang!*' Kira yelled, her stomach tightening as she realised just how big the snake was. '*Fang! Kill it! Kill it!*'

Heavy and strong though the snake was, it was no match for Longfang. The dragon's jaws had gained a good purchase. With brutal efficiency he clamped them tighter and tighter, his teeth shearing through the snake's flesh and crushing its spine. With a savage twist of his neck, Fang bit the enormous snake in two. For a heartbeat the two halves thrashed and twisted, the great muscles reacting to autonomic triggers before gradually going limp.

Fang's head rose as the snake dropped from his neck. He appeared to be chewing.

'*Are you all right?*' Kira asked aloud.

'*I am perfectly fine, Kira. I always was partial to a bit of snake meat. Very tasty,*' he said, tossing his head as he swallowed the great chunk of snake. '*I've not seen one this big for a very long time. It will make for a good meal.*'

'He's all right,' Kira told the others, trying to sound casual. Nolita was pale with shock and Elian did not look a lot better. 'We'd better be on our guard tonight. Fang tells me the orb is giving off a blood scent that's attracting predators. The dragons will keep watch, but we might want to hold a watch of our own as well.'

'I'd say that's not a bad idea,' Elian agreed.

The night passed without further incident. The dragons positioned their bodies to form a protective circle around the riders' shelter. The proximity

25

of the dragons set Nolita shaking, but she was so exhausted from her trial earlier in the day that, despite her reaction and the shock of the snake attack, she was quick to sink into a deep sleep. Kira volunteered to take the first watch and quickly realised the steps the dragons had taken made her efforts redundant. When the time came for Elian to begin his watch, rather than wake him, she slipped into the shelter alongside him and left the dragons to their vigil.

## Chapter Three
# The Hunter's Instinct

On waking to the eerie light of pre-dawn, Kira was glad that she had decided not to keep the watch going. They had all benefited from a good sleep and there was no telling what time of day or night it might be on the far side of the gateway. The other world that Aurora took them to was frightening. It was a place of war and danger unlike anywhere in Areth. They all needed their wits about them to negotiate it safely and get back to the Oracle with the orb.

The sudden roar of a big cat made her sit up straight. It sounded close. For an instant her mind flashed back to the first time she had heard that noise.

*'Don't worry, Kira. It knows better than to come*

*any closer.'* Fang's voice in her mind was calm and measured.

She didn't reply, but was reassured by Fang's presence. The feeling triggered memories of her first overnight trip into the savannah, and Manoush, the hunter who had taken her. He had inspired similar feelings of safety. A fond smile crept across her face. Despite the hunter's status, everyone in the village called him Moo because of his size and leisurely gait.

He had never walked like the other hunters. Where they stalked warily through the long grass and bushes, Moo moved in a gently meandering fashion, unthreatening and slow. His big brown eyes, wide face and huge torso portrayed a certain resemblance to the village cows, but his appearance was deceptive. Moo was one of the most successful hunters in her tribe. He was also a maverick. Other hunters did not like working with him, despite his frequent successes.

Kira was delighted when Moo suggested the overnight trip to her parents. He convinced them by suggesting that if she were sufficiently frightened by the experience, she might decide to give up on the idea of becoming a hunter and turn her attention to something more appropriate for a girl of her age. Her father had been grateful to the big man, not suspecting for a moment that Moo had no intention of allowing her to get frightened – quite the opposite.

The strange hunter had shown her many useful hunting tricks, and with his hulking presence at her side she had learned to respect the dangers of the night without fearing them. Even the roaring of the lions as dawn broke had been more fascinating than frightening. When the big man dropped her off at the family hut the next morning, her father expected her to be a quivering wreck. He could barely conceal his anger when she bubbled with enthusiasm over the experience. She could still picture Moo's sly wink to her the moment her father's back had turned. He was a good man, was Moo.

A horrible thought suddenly crossed her mind. If the orb was drawing predators to them here in Areth, what sort of attention would it attract in the other world? The warmth of her memories died in an instant and icy needles shot through her belly. 'Best not to think about that too hard,' she told herself.

They all had a quick wash at the water's edge, under the watchful eyes of the three dragons. Then it was time to gather their things and mount up before the sun broke the horizon.

'Are you sure you're going to be all right riding alone, Nolita?' Elian asked.

'I'll manage,' she mumbled. 'If I'm ever going to get over my fears, I need to keep working at it.'

Kira gave her an encouraging pat on the shoulder. Nolita impressed her more with every passing day. Elian did not look convinced, but Kira stared at him until he backed off and resumed packing his gear. He was acting like a mother hen. Nolita had a full set of flying gear now, so even if they emerged from the gate into the freezing air of high altitude like last time, she would be prepared. Firestorm would look after her.

There was no sign of the snake's carcass, but the contented feeling she sensed from Fang told her all she needed to know. If he had not eaten the snake by himself, the dragons had shared it. She shuddered. They were welcome to it. Snake meat had never been a favourite. It was not the flavour. It was the thought of what she was eating that put her off. So much for the hardened hunter, she thought, with an inward grimace.

They mounted their dragons. Nolita looked pale as a wraith in the milky morning light. In contrast, Firestorm's blue scales were vibrant. His delight at his rider's continued bravery reflected in his proud stance and sparkling eyes. He was almost unrecognisable from the washed-out dragon they had first met a week before, when Nolita was too scared to go near him.

Elian indicated for Kira to take the lead on Fang. As they launched, accelerating into the take-off with an explosion of speed, Kira caught sight of several lions scattering from their flight path. This might be their normal hunting territory, but Kira suspected the orb was more likely to be the reason for their presence. The dragons were a powerful deterrent, but a group of large predators in full blood-frenzy could prove dangerous. The sooner they got rid of the orb, the better.

The familiar sight of the swirling grey vortex ahead of them caused Kira to hold her breath. These gateways that Aurora formed were very useful, but most unpleasant to enter. In that final instant before crossing the threshold, Kira wished that she did not have to enter first. She knew the order they had decided upon was logical, but that did not make it any easier. Aurora had to be last because the gateway would collapse behind her the instant she entered. Nolita had only ever been through the gateways whilst riding with Elian on Aurora until now. It would not be fair to ask her and Firestorm to lead the way. Nolita was not up to that yet.

They entered, plunging into nothingness. The strange twisting wrench no longer troubled her, but Kira hated the sensation that followed. It felt as though she was submerged in a liquid, floating in grey nothingness. The feeling always made her think of death. Was this what it would be like after she breathed her last? She hoped not. She could not think of anything worse.

The second wrench on emergence into the other world was disorienting, but she was happy to be in clear air again. It was dark and cold here. Kira looked around. The others had emerged behind her. She could not see them, but the powerful wingbeats of Firestorm and Aurora were distinctly audible.

'Where are we, Fang?' she asked silently.

'We're not far from where we emerged last time,' he replied. 'The human battle-lines are almost directly beneath us. Aurora is going to lead us back to the woods where we hid before.'

Bursts of light to their right suddenly lit up the countryside with a rapid sequence of spectacular flashes. Thumping cracks followed quickly, the sounds splitting the air in a way that seemed to tear at the very fabric of reality. Kira's stomach felt as if it were in her throat as her eyes automatically flicked from one eruption of fire to the next.

The noise of the explosions caused details of previous visits to zip through her mind in a rapid sequence of images: the strange flying machines that had attacked them, the brave airman who had flown to their aid and the terrible aerial conflict that had followed. Would they see the man again? It seemed unlikely. Even if he were nearby, the darkness would cloak him.

The dragons were flying low enough to pick out some details during the brief moments of illumination. The trenches were distinctly visible: long lines gouged deep into the earth, a mesmerising pattern of wounds. There were people down there – many thousands of people. How could they do this day after day? How long had they been fighting? Kira could find no sense in it.

Aurora took the lead and veered off to the west, away from the seemingly endless trenches. Elian's dragon was right. The woods were a good place to hide.

'*How long until sunrise, Fang?*'

'*About an hour and a half,*' the dragon replied. '*Aurora's senses are finely attuned to the moment of dawn.*'

'*Not long, then. Good,*' Kira said. Although Aurora's ability to travel to this world was useful, the elapsed time between worlds did not match in any measurable way, so there was no way of knowing how long they would have to spend here. Gateways could only be formed at dawn in either world. Aurora could control when she arrived in Areth, but she could not tell what time of day or night it would be until she emerged through the gateway into this other world. The less time we spend here, the better, Kira thought.

'*I've got a bad feeling about tonight,*' she continued. '*Stay alert, Fang. My hunter's instinct is prickling.*'

The dragon did not respond verbally to her warning, but she could feel his increased concentration. He was reaching out with his senses. Despite the concealing blanket of the dark night sky, she also felt him camouflage. It was disconcerting when he effectively disappeared from beneath her, especially at night.

As they moved further from the lines of fighting, so the constant noise of battle reduced to a distant rumble. The dragons slowly descended, dropping lower and lower until Kira found she could make out certain shapes on the ground. It was a dark night, but her eyes had adjusted to the low light and she could see farmhouses, trees and the line of a river. The sound of a dog barking was just audible above the wind-rush. Kira smiled. There no telling what had disturbed the dog but, if it was reacting to their presence, she did not think the animal would be so brave if it were to meet the dragons.

They landed next to the woods and as soon as the riders had dismounted, the dragons moved between the trees towards the little clearing where they had camped during their previous visit. Leaves were piling up beneath the tangled branches and the rich earthy smell of the autumn mulch filled the air. Looking back, she saw a faint edge of frost tinging the grass in the field where they had touched down.

Kira had barely taken a couple of paces before she noticed. She removed a glove, held her hand in front of her mouth and breathed over it. She was breathing smoke! Her breath felt warm. Why was she breathing smoke? Was this a side effect of being a dragonrider? Momentary panic set her heart racing and she looked around at the others to see if either of them had noticed. They were breathing out smoke as well. Elian had a look of wonder on his face as he experimented just as she had. Nolita, though, did not look in the slightest bit perturbed.

Should I tell her? Kira wondered. She doesn't appear to have noticed.

As if she had somehow heard Kira's thoughts,

Nolita turned to look first at her and then at Elian.

'What's the matter?' she asked softly. 'You look as if you've seen a ghost.'

'My breath!' Elian whispered. 'It's smoking.'

To Kira's surprise, Nolita began to chuckle, more smoke puffing from between her lips.

'Are you telling me you've never seen your breath before?' Nolita laughed, struggling to keep her voice down. 'Don't you have winter in Racafi? Doesn't it get cold enough for you to see your breath?'

'We have different seasons, but it never gets this cold,' Kira replied. 'Is this normal, then?'

'Perfectly normal,' Nolita said, making a face and deliberately breathing out through her nose. The smoke-like vapour coiled lazily from her nostrils. 'What do you think? Could I be an honorary dragon?'

For Nolita to make such a joke was both extraordinary and unexpectedly funny. Kira began to snigger and Elian was quick to join her. They turned together and began to follow the dragons through the trees, all the while asking questions about Nolita's experience of winter in Cemaria.

There was something satisfying about scrunching through the thick layer of leaves. It was all but impossible to move silently, so Kira didn't try.

Instead she deliberately kicked through the piles, the sensation bringing a strange sense of exuberance. It was not long until dawn. Their first success seemed close and it felt good.

They had reached the edge of the clearing where the dragons were already settling down to wait when something set the hairs prickling at the back of Kira's neck again. She stopped suddenly and tipped her head slightly to listen.

'What is it, Kira?' Elian's voice was suddenly empty of humour.

'Shh! Stand still – both of you. Listen!'

Nothing. The distant rumble of war was constant, but aside from that disconcerting backdrop of sound the night was still. After a long pause, Kira shook her head and grinned.

'Sorry,' she said. 'That snake must have messed with my instincts. I keep getting the feeling something bad is about to happen. Did you see those lions when we left? Do you think they were being drawn to the orb?'

Elian shrugged and Nolita paled still further.

'If the orb's influence is that strong, maybe we should prepare for trouble,' Kira continued. 'With all the blood being spilled in the trenches, I doubt it will attract much interest, but there's no harm in being careful.'

'I can't argue with that,' Elian replied, his expression thoughtful. 'What do you suggest?'

'Let's get the dragons to form a circle around us as they did last night. We'll mount up a little earlier than normal and get into position to leave as soon as Aurora can form a gateway.'

'Sounds sensible.'

The dragons agreed. Once inside the protective circle formed by their scaly flanks, Kira began to relax. The three riders huddled together for warmth, but it made little difference. Their layers of protective clothing masked any benefits and the cold slowly seeped into their limbs. Before long they were all walking around in the circular hollow, stamping their feet and waving their arms to stimulate blood flow.

Time dragged, every minute stretching out into an age as dawn stubbornly refused to break. Kira began to think the night would never end. Looking at the others, she could see they were having similar thoughts. It was the sound of the first dog barking that brought her to an abrupt standstill. Elian cocked his head for a moment and then continued his efforts to warm himself as soon as he had identified the sound.

'What's the matter, Kira?' he asked. 'It's just a dog.'

Kira's nerves were tingling all down her back. Was this it? Did the dog's barking herald the danger she had sensed since they first landed? A second dog added its bark to the first. That was enough. Kira turned to the others.

'Mount up!' she ordered abruptly.

'What?' Elian exclaimed. 'Don't be silly, Kira. What threat are a couple of dogs?'

'We're being hunted. We need to get out of here now.'

Her tone held such authority that there were no further questions. Elian knew better than to challenge her when she spoke with that voice, and Nolita was always happier when given directions. The three riders scrambled up the sides of their dragons.

'*The dogs are coming closer, Kira,*' Fang warned. '*And there are lots of them,*' he added. He sounded surprised and Kira could not blame him. Dragons were used to being respected and feared by all members of the animal kingdom, with a few very unusual exceptions. More and more dogs were adding their voices to the pack. Their frenzied barking held no respect for anything. They were closing fast.

'We need to get into the open,' Kira called. 'We should get into the air and fly until the sun comes up. There's no space for the dragons to take off here, so let's get back to the field where we landed.'

'No arguments here,' Elian called back.

The dragons had to go carefully. Moving through the trees on their own was one thing, but they did not want their riders to be swept from their saddles by low branches.

They had barely entered the trees when the first of the dogs came running towards them, attacking in a ferocious, mindless pack of slavering, snarling teeth and fur. They were all shapes and sizes, from great lumbering canine brutes right down through the scale to animals barely bigger than rats that yapped and snarled around the legs of their bigger cousins. Had the dragons been in the open, the dogs would have posed little threat. Dragon scales were impervious to the teeth and nails of the canine attackers. Hampered by the trees, however, the riders were in danger. There was little the dragons could do but try to ignore the dogs and push forwards towards the open fields nearby.

Although some dogs leaped at Kira, snapping at her legs with vicious teeth and madness in their eyes, the majority of the pack focused their attention on Firestorm and Nolita. The day dragon all but disappeared as the dogs swept around him. Kira could see that Nolita had drawn her legs right up and was now kneeling on the saddle, precariously balanced and quite understandably terrified.

It must be the orb, Kira thought. *Its influence here seems to be magnified. It's driving the poor creatures insane.*

'*Hang on, Kira,*' Fang warned. '*And close your eyes. Firestorm is about to warm things up.*'

'What's he going to do?' she asked aloud.

Fang did not have time to answer before she found out. The brave blue dragon lifted his head, cracking the branches above with ease before filling the air ahead of him with a great burst of roaring fire that consumed everything in its path. Firestorm barely paused before pushing forwards into the smouldering passage he had blasted through the trees. Nolita ducked her head down between her arms and clamped her eyes tight shut.

'Great gods!' Kira breathed. She had been slow to close her eyes and a glaring after-image of Firestorm's fiery breath burned yellow on her retinas. 'Everyone within about three leagues will have seen that. *Quick, Fang! Follow Firestorm. We have to get out of here, now!*'

## Chapter Four
# A Painful Awakening

Everything hurt. Pell's mind recoiled from the sensation, shrinking inwards in an effort to ward off the pain. It felt as though bones were broken in every area of his body. He wondered if he should try to move. Even breathing sent sharp spikes through his chest.

Bracing himself mentally, he tried to move his arm. Red agony exploded through the tensed muscles and he groaned, the noise triggering yet more pain. It was excruciating, but despite his foolishness he was alive. Pain could be overcome. Injuries would heal. However, time was pressing. The Oracle needed him to act quickly.

He opened his eyes. There was a ceiling above him. It looked rough and unfinished, but sound. He was in a bed. How had he come to be in a bed?

The last thing he remembered was the impact of Shadow's talons.

'*You're awake!*'

'*Shadow?*' he croaked.

'Mama! Mama, he's awake!'

The voice was that of a little girl. She sounded both excited and a little frightened.

'Shush now, Saffi. Don't disturb 'im. He needs to rest. Run along now.' The woman's voice was gentle and warm, but as soon as Pell saw her, he found her body language was at odds with her tone. The woman's dark eyes were narrowed and her lips twisted with intense dislike. Her arms were tightly folded across her chest and her torso was half turned away in a stance that suggested defiance. She was stout and prim, with her hair tied in a tight bun at the back of her head.

Pell caught sight of a little girl in a plain dress as she disappeared out through the door.

'Did I do something wrong?' he whispered.

'I dunno,' the woman responded immediately, her voice suddenly hard and uncaring. 'Did you? We've seen your kind before. We know what you're like.'

'*Your kind?* What do you mean?' he asked, his mind spinning.

'Dark riders on your black dragons –

troublemakers, the lot of yous,' she said fiercely. Her eyebrows drew together in an angry frown. 'Well you don't frighten me. Your dragon dropped you on me doorstep. I saw you was hurt and I don't turn away the needy, no matter who they be. But as soon as you can move, you're leavin'. Understand?'

'Yes,' he replied softly.

He was in no fit state for a discussion, but he resolved to find out why night dragonriders had such a bad reputation here. This was not the first time he had experienced such hostility. In some places it seemed that whenever trouble or misfortune struck, night dragons became the scapegoats.

Pell thought Shadow was a beautiful dragon, but he knew that many considered her appearance frightening. Some even felt she looked evil. He and Shadow had met two season rotations ago. Since that time they had never caused anyone harm, yet on several occasions they had been accused of stealing livestock, or damaging property. It's so unfair, he thought. People are so shallow. They never look for the good in others. I'll bet her attitude would be different if Shadow was a day dragon.

'You want food?' the woman asked.

'Yes, please,' Pell answered. Anything to speed

my recovery and get me away from you, he added silently.

'Ain't got much, but it'll have to serve.'

She left, closing the door firmly behind her. As soon as the door closed, Pell relaxed into the bed. He had not felt his body tense up, but the relief he felt as she left surprised him with its intensity.

'*You'll be well soon,*' Shadow assured him. '*Eat. Rest. Your body heals fast. We'll be on our way before you know it.*'

'*Thanks, Shadow. And thanks for catching me. I won't ever be able to thank you enough for that.*'

Shadow didn't respond, but he could feel her pleasure through their special bond. She would be sharing his pain, just as he shared in her delight. The bond was a curious thing. At times it felt tenuous, like a filament of wispy smoke, nebulous and faint. At other times, though – like now – it felt strong and solid, like an iron bridge between their minds across which thoughts and feelings flowed back and forth in a constant stream.

Although they had only been together for two rotations, it was hard to remember what it had been like before they met. Pell had never been one to enjoy close friendships with his peers. He was too much like his father – strong, silent and solitary by nature. His mother was warmer, but with her husband out in the forest most of the time, she had been forced into the role of the disciplinarian. Three strong boys and a wilful girl had needed a firm hand to control. Pell's two brothers were too competitive to be close, and he did not want to be seen as weak in their eyes for spending time with his sister. But now no one would ever think him weak, because of his close relationship with Shadow. Now he had her, he felt no need to become close to anyone else. She was everything to him, and together they would achieve more than his siblings would ever have dreamed possible.

The woman returned with a tray and placed it on a small table next to his bed. On it there was a hunk of bread, a cup of milk and a bowl of steaming broth. Pell tried to move again, but it was too painful. To his embarrassment, the woman grabbed him under his armpits and hauled him up into a sitting position. The movement was incredibly painful, but aside from drawing a sharp intake of breath, he said nothing.

'Can you manage, or does you want me to feed you?' she asked, moving the tray to his lap.

'I'll be all right,' he mumbled, adding his thanks.

She nodded. 'I'll be back in a bit. Don't let Saffi bother you. I've told her not to come in here, but if she does sneak in then do us a favour and send her away, would you?'

Pell nodded. So I can't corrupt her with my dark ways, no doubt, he thought grimly, keeping his suspicions to himself. The woman's prejudice bothered him, but he was determined to remain civil. Rather than dwell on it, he concentrated on the tray of food. The bread was not fresh, but neither could it yet be called stale. The vegetable stew looked watery, but the steamy scent rising from it smelled good. Pell took a bite from the bread and sipped some milk from the cup. The milk was nicely chilled and the bread reduced to a heavenly paste in his mouth.

Alternating between dunking the bread in the steaming vegetable broth and eating it with sips of milk, he slowly consumed everything on the tray. By the time he was finished he felt exhausted, and waves of pain washed up and down his body with a cruel rhythm. As she had promised, the woman returned a short while later. She removed the empty tray and helped make him comfortable again. Pell barely managed to mumble his thanks before sleep dragged him down into its deep dark well.

When he next surfaced, Pell felt much better. Bracing himself against the anticipated spikes of agony, he tentatively raised his right arm a few finger-widths above the blankets. It hurt, but nothing like it had earlier. Heartened, he tested his body further, moving first one limb, then the next. Having tried them all, he eased himself up into a sitting position. As he did so, his head spun and he teetered on the brink of passing out. The moment passed. His head cleared. He blinked a few times to clear the remnants of sleep from his eyes.

The sheets fell from his torso and he realised that he was bare to his waist. By twisting his head, Pell could just see the great lines of purple across his back. Shadow must have hit him pretty hard to cause such vivid bruising, he realised. He had no way of telling whether he had suffered any internal injuries, but he sensed he must have been lucky.

His clothes were draped over a nearby chair. Taking care not to stand up too quickly, Pell eased himself up to his feet. With tentative, shuffling steps he crossed the short distance from the bed to the chair. Getting his shirt over his head was a struggle, but somehow he managed it. The effort left him breathless for some time.

'*Are you all right?*' Shadow asked, her voice full of concern.

'I'll be fine,' he replied. '*I'm going to finish dressing, see if the woman has any more food and then we'll get out of here.*'

'That would be wonderful, but are you sure it's wise? I feel the pull of the Oracle's mission, Pell, but I can also feel your pain. I'm not convinced you're well enough to travel yet.'

'I'm not staying in this house one heartbeat longer than necessary, Shadow. Didn't you hear the poison in her tone last time she spoke to me? The woman hates me. She hates you. She hates having me here. I don't want to give that hatred time to stew. I'd like to put some distance between us and this place by nightfall.'

'I'll be waiting for you outside,' she assured him.

Tears welled in his eyes as he struggled into his flying trousers, and the weight of his jacket hung heavy on his shoulders. The most difficult challenge, however, was his boots. The combination of bending and pulling proved too difficult. No matter how hard he tried, Pell could not get his feet into them properly. Eventually, he let out a cry of frustration, mingled with pain, that brought his hostess running.

'What d'you think you're doin'?' she asked, bustling over to the bed and sitting him upright. She knelt by his feet and pulled off the boot that was halfway onto his right foot.

'Getting out of your life,' he replied. 'Help me on with my boots and I'll be on my way.'

'What's the matter with you? Gotta death wish,

49

or somethin'? You'd have to be crazy to try'n fly, state you're in.'

'Crazy?' He laughed. 'Maybe I am, missus. But I'm going anyway. I've got to. I made a promise. No matter what you think of me, my word is good. Please, help me on with my boots. There's money in my saddlebag. I won't see you out of pocket on my behalf, but I must leave now.'

The woman looked up at him, her dark eyes narrowed once more. This time, however, her gaze was more thoughtful than hostile. She regarded him for a few heartbeats before making up her mind.

'Very well, young master. I'll help you into your boots and send you on your way. But you're not leavin' without havin' a bite more to eat before you go. I insist.'

'Thank you. That would be most kind.'

Pell was glad to accept her offer. His stomach was rumbling and the little food he had in his saddlebags was past its best. He would need to buy more supplies soon. He had a fair amount of money, but not enough to last long. He and Shadow would need to earn more at a town or city soon, unless they were to live off the land.

Money was easy enough to come by when you had a dragon's abilities to trade. Authorities were always happy to pay to have a dragon determine whether those accused of crimes were guilty, or innocent. The draconic ability to search a man's mind for the truth was renowned, if somewhat exaggerated. It saved the judiciary a huge amount of time and expense. Shadow had made several such judgements since they had been together. She had claimed confidence in her decision each time, but Pell had some doubts about her ability to be one hundred per cent sure. Despite their special mental link he felt certain that he could hide things from her if he wanted to, so he found himself questioning how she could determine the truth in the minds of others.

To Pell's thinking, moving trees, or other heavy objects, was far more honest work. Shadow did not like it as much. She felt the work to be demeaning. But when funds were low, it offered a good source of income. A dragon's strength was greater than the combined power of several horses. Not only this, but the dragon's intelligence meant that if you asked a dragon to move something, it was moved to exactly where you wanted it.

With his boots on, Pell felt more stable on his feet. He followed the woman to the door, moving more easily with almost every step. The little girl, Saffi, was waiting as he stepped through into the next room.

'Hey, mister! Is your dragon goin' to eat old Strumble?'

'Now don't start your pesterin', Saffi. If you wants to stay, you'll have to promise not to bother him.'

Pell looked at the little girl's rebellious face and decided to answer, despite the mother's admonition. 'Strumble?' he asked, giving her a smile. 'I doubt it. Shadow doesn't need to eat as often as we do. She only ate yesterday, so we'll be long gone before she needs to eat again. Who is old Strumble, anyway?'

The little girl's face displayed a mixture of relief and disappointment. 'Strumble's our cow, mister. An evil old heffer, she is. Stamp on your foot as soon as look at you she would. An' she's not light, despite her bein' skinny.'

*'Actually I last ate two days ago, but you can assure her that the cow is safe. I wouldn't touch that old bag of bones unless I was starving,'* Shadow told him.

'Shadow tells me she's not interested in eating your cow,' Pell assured her gently. 'She likes to hunt in the wilds. The meat is tastier.' He looked around as if checking to see if anyone were looking, and dropped his voice to a secretive whisper. 'Between you and me, I think she's a bit fussy about her food. She says she can taste the difference, but I think she's making it up.'

Shadow's loud snort from outside the window set the little girl giggling, her hands covering her mouth.

'*The difference is marked to anyone with a sense of taste,*' Shadow huffed.

'*Just playing to my audience,*' Pell replied innocently, not speaking aloud.

'You're all right, mister,' Saffi announced in a loud voice. 'Your dragon's a bit scary, but you're all right.'

'Thank you, Saffi. I'm glad you think so.'

And he *was* glad. It felt good to be accepted. So why did he find it so hard to integrate into the dragonrider community? It was strange. At home he had always been accepted by his siblings and popular with his peers, but from the moment he met Shadow his relationships with them had changed. His surge of ambition had isolated him from everyone he had held dear. He still found it easy to charm those from whom he sensed no challenge, but amongst his peers he became insular and cold.

Was he wrong to be ambitious? He and Shadow were a formidable partnership. He could *feel* their potential as a team. The fall, humbling as it had been, had left him feeling more complete. When the leaders of the night dragon enclave learned he had embarked on the Great Quest, his standing would rise rapidly.

Riders from other enclaves did not trust the night dragons. Therefore, he could not afford to trust them. It was wrong that dragons should be judged by appearance, but there was a distinct prejudice. It was present both amongst the general populace, and amongst the rest of the dragonrider community. Night dragons looked particularly fierce with their heavily armoured bodies, their sharp horns and red eyes. Because of this, folk were quick to blame no end of ills on them.

It's time that changed, he thought. It'll take a while, but it's a goal worth striving for.

## Chapter Five
# A Confident Guess

Glowing embers and the smouldering remains of twigs and smaller branches dripped from the trees in a red, smoking rain. Steam hissed from the damp, leafy carpet like a thousand snakes. The yelps of pain and fright from those unfortunate dogs singed by spark or flame were lost amongst the frenzied barking of the main pack.

Nolita had been ready for the blast of fire. Firestorm had given her a timely warning. She held her breath, curled into a tight ball on her saddle and tucked her head between her forearms as she clung to the pommel with all her strength.

'*Hang on tight, Nolita. We're getting out of here.*'

Nolita didn't reply to her dragon's order. Instead she kept her head low and, ignoring the danger from the dogs leaping and scrabbling at Firestorm's flanks, she slipped her feet down into the stirrups. It was well that she did, for the added stability kept her from falling as her dragon shot forwards through the smoke-filled tunnel under the trees.

Unable to hold her breath any longer, she drew in a gulping gasp. The thick smoke instantly irritated the back of her throat, triggering an involuntary fit of coughing. Panic gripped her afresh as she lost control of her breathing. Nolita felt she had gained some mastery over her fear during the last few days, but a familiar wall of blackness was looming. Her head spun as she flirted with unconsciousness. Being on Firestorm's back brought fear enough, but the concentrated attack by the dogs had raised her fear levels to new heights. Now she was not only on a dragon's back, but smoke-blind, choking, and racing through a treacherous, burning tunnel under the trees. It was hard to imagine anything more terrifying.

Even as Firestorm ran forwards, she felt him draw in another deep breath. The roar as he sent a second blast of flame ahead of them was not unexpected, but the wash of heat was so intense that she wondered if some of the smell of burning that filled her mouth, nose and throat was that of her own hair.

'*Stay with me, Nolita,*' Fire urged. '*Nearly there. One more blast will see us clear.*'

She forced her eyes open a crack, but she couldn't make sense of what she was seeing. He was preparing to spew another gout of fire. She could feel him gathering it beneath her. She clamped her eyelids tight shut again. A moment later and a third roar issued from his throat. The mindless barking of the dogs was beginning to fall behind them now. Suddenly she felt the change of air. They were clear of the trees. She felt Firestorm's muscles bunch as he extended his wings and began his first downstroke.

The whoosh of air that marked the beginning of Firestorm's take-off brought a sense of relief. A few days ago it would have amplified her fear, but the increasingly familiar rhythmic feeling as they launched into the air served this time to calm her. They had escaped the pack. Her coughing began to subside. Fresh air forced the smoke from her lungs, but the taste of it remained as she started to regain control of her breathing.

A sharp series of cracking reports were followed an instant later by a stinging sensation in her chest. It took a moment to realise that the pain it brought was not hers, but Firestorm's. She was feeling it through their mental link. The sound of something whizzing through the air helped her identify the source of the noise. Someone was directing one of

57

the strange weapons of this world in their direction. More cracking noises announced the release of more weapons, but none found their mark.

'*We're clear,*' Fire announced. '*The others are safe. They are right behind us.*'

'*Thank you,*' she replied, feeling guilty. Nolita had been so caught up in her own predicament that she had not spared a thought for her companions. Tears of relief replaced those caused by the smoke. She twisted her head to dash them from her cheeks with her shoulder. Letting go of the pommel to wipe them away with her hand was still beyond her.

With a final hacking cough she cleared her throat. 'I felt that weapon hit you, Fire,' she said aloud. 'Are you all right?'

'*I'm fine, Nolita,*' he replied, clearly touched by her concern. '*It stings a little, but it did not penetrate my scales.*'

'Good,' she said. And to her amazement, she found that she meant it. It was barely more than a week ago that Elian and Kira had tied her to Aurora's saddle and whisked into this quest. Revulsion and terror had been her dominant emotions then, but now she cared about this great, fire-breathing beast. Its appearance still frightened her. Its ability to communicate directly with her mind still felt alien and uncomfortable, but despite everything she was developing positive feelings for him that she would never have believed possible just a short time ago.

She looked around. As they climbed, the pre-dawn light was increasing. The silhouette of Aurora's sleek form was clearly visible a little behind and to the right. She could see no sign of Fang and Kira, but that was not unusual. Fang's camouflage made him totally invisible in this light, and Kira's slim form was not easy to see.

'*We're going to keep climbing,*' Fire informed her. '*Aside from being safer, the dawn will come more quickly the higher we get.*'

'*Really?*' Nolita replied. '*Why's that? Surely the sun isn't affected by our flying.*'

'No,' Fire chuckled. '*Dragons have many abilities, but we cannot move the sun. Would that we could, for then Aurora's dawn window would be easy to meet. No, it's all to do with angles. I'll explain it to you sometime if you like.*'

'*Angles? Thank you, no. My brother, Balard, tried to explain angles to me last year, Fire. I developed a headache faster than you'd believe possible. I don't think I have the right sort of mind for clever stuff like that.*'

'*I think you might be surprised at what you can learn if you try, Nolita, now that your mind is less clouded by fear. There are many things that you could excel at if you put your mind to them.'*

'*Really?*' she said, wondering what sorts of things the dragon felt she might be good at. The strange mental bridge that linked their minds drew her. She had shied away from it until now, choosing to shout across the link rather than explore it. But the bridge between their minds was not going to go away. It was another of the boundaries marking the edge of her comfort zone. Could she direct her thoughts across the bridge? What would she find on the other side? Would she be able to read Firestorm's thoughts?

The last few days had taught her some of the benefits of confronting her fears. With a sense of trepidation, she probed the bond with tentative exploratory thought. It felt strange to touch the link in this way – uncomfortable, but sort of exciting. It reminded her of when she had secretly searched the house for midwinter gifts as a little girl. The delicious mixture of excitement and the danger of being caught by her parents was unforgettable. She had never discovered where her mother concealed the gifts, but the thrill of the search had stayed with her.

Her experience this time was different. Where she had failed in her goal as a child, this time she succeeded. Her gentle tendril of thought crossed the bridge into Firestorm's mind. With a gasp, she withdrew it immediately.

It took a moment for her to understand what she had seen. The sensation in that alien environment had been one of vastness, like the Chamber of the Sun's Steps, but much, much bigger. More, there had been a pervading sense of wisdom and knowledge that spanned back over many season rotations. As she tried to resolve the experience into an image she could relate to, a picture of a great library formed – a huge storehouse of knowledge that stretched into the distance in all directions.

Firestorm did not say anything, but she knew he had felt her presence in his mind. The bond now carried a flavour of welcome. A shudder ran down her spine. Despite the silent welcome being offered by the dragon, she recoiled from the idea of crossing again.

The temperature was dropping fast as they climbed through a small gap in the clouds. Her last glimpse of the shadowy, patchwork landscape below was one of strange tranquillity. The steady beating of Firestorm's wings and the whisper of their passage through the air were the only sounds audible. When she considered the horrors of the war below and the terrible weapons with which it was being fought, it was hard to reconcile the peaceful image with the reality.

Nolita did not have to be warned of the imminence of dawn. It was obvious. In the moment that the swirling grey vortex appeared ahead of them, she fought down the flash of panic with the ease of regular recent practice. They plunged into the swirling void, the gut-wrenching twist and the sense of weightlessness now familiar enough to be more uncomfortable than terrifying. Emergence into the air amongst the mountains of Orupee was more frightening.

On her last visit here the wind across the mountaintops had subjected Nolita and the others to dangerous turbulence and vicious air currents. This time the air was smooth, but filled with a murky mist of rain that offered a different kind of danger. Nolita could see the ground directly below, but horizontal visibility was limited in all directions to no more than a few dragon lengths. At the speed they were flying it would be easy to fly into a cliff-face before being able to react to its presence.

'*Can we slow down?*' she asked.

'*Not easily,*' Firestorm replied. '*Dragons are not too good at hovering. Our wings are not well suited to that sort of flying. We can do it for a second or two in times of need, but it takes vast amounts of energy.*

Our wings are better suited to cruising at high speed.'

'Well, can we descend, then? It looks clearer down there,' she pointed out.

'We can try, but it won't be any better,' Fire told her. 'It's an optical illusion, Nolita. If we go down, we will increase the likelihood of running into a ridge, or an outcrop of rock. At least up here we just have mountaintops to worry about.'

'Just the mountaintops! You're not filling me with confidence, Fire. How will we find the Oracle's cave?'

'I'm going to make a guess.'

'Guess! Are you mad?' Nolita's voice cracked on the last syllable.

'No, not mad,' he assured her. 'Just very confident of my guesses. When we flew along this valley last time, I memorised some of the landmarks and their relative positions. It's a habit. All dragons do it to one degree or another. I happen to be quite good at it.'

Nolita's stomach churned as she squinted into the misty rain. Having experienced a momentary flash of the dragon's mind, she could well imagine him memorising landmarks. However, the idea that he could reference those landmarks with sufficient accuracy to safely navigate the treacherous path she remembered was simply not believable.

Visions of looming cliffs filled her mind. If they did hit a rock wall she had no illusions of her chances of survival. A dragon was tough – maybe Firestorm would have a chance. She would have none. The valley floor was many hundreds of spans below. No human could survive a fall like that. Her hands clenched yet tighter around the pommel of her saddle.

The ethereal white-grey mist muffled the rhythmic whooshing sound of the dragons' wingbeats. We could be anywhere, Nolita thought, her mind racing. The rain caressed with a touch like the finest silk across her cheeks and forehead. Gradually it beaded, moistening her lips and running into her eyes. The other dragons, even when flying in close formation, were blurry ghostlike figures: gigantic sinister shadows – the stuff of her nightmares.

Seconds dragged into minutes. Minutes sapped the energy of hours. And every instant Nolita felt sure would be her last.

*'We're there.'*

Firestorm's announcement coincided with an abrupt change of wingbeat rhythm that nearly threw Nolita from the saddle. The dragon suddenly reared in the sky as a grey wall of rock loomed ahead of them. To Nolita's amazement, just three rapid wingbeats slowed them sufficiently to allow them to land softly on the ledge directly in front of the Oracle's cave.

'How on Areth did you manage that?' she gasped in amazement.

'*I cheated,*' Firestorm admitted with a mental chuckle. '*The Oracle draws dragons who have a reason to visit it, but I refined the instinctive pull by seeking ahead with my mind for the Guardians. The dragons who stand watch at the entrance to the Oracle's cave with their riders were content to allow me to use their minds like a homing beacon. It was this, combined with my memory of the terrain, that got us here safely.*'

'Next time you decide to get clever, I'd appreciate it if you'd let me in on your tricks, Fire,' Nolita muttered through gritted teeth. 'I was convinced I was going to die from the moment we emerged from the gateway. Flying is frightening enough when I can see what's going on.'

'*Sorry, Nolita,*' he replied, contrite. '*I was concentrating so hard on where we were going that I hadn't noticed your discomfort was greater than usual.*'

Fang and Aurora had also landed beside them. Kira and Elian were already dismounting, so Nolita forced her fingers to release their death grip on the pommel of her saddle. She grabbed the orb from her saddlebag and carefully slid down Fire's side to join her companions on the ledge. They moved quickly forwards into the mouth of the great cave, with the dragons following close behind.

Once again the Guardians stepped out of their alcoves on each side of the tunnel, but as soon as they saw the orb in Nolita's hands they ushered the party forwards. The great cavern where they had encountered the Oracle last time seemed a shade darker than Nolita remembered, but as they descended towards the wall around the vast, circular, well-like chasm, she decided it must be her overactive imagination. There were just as many torches lining the walls as there had been during their previous visit. It was most likely the after-effects of flying through the whiteness of the misty cloud.

The party reached the wall that surrounded the Oracle's great pit and they stopped. There was a breathless air of anticipation in the chamber, but nothing happened. No swirling smoke. No sign of the Oracle. Heartbeat after heartbeat passed, but nothing happened.

'Great! What are we supposed to do now?' Nolita muttered.

Tembo's eyes were quick to focus on Husam as he sensed the man straighten up. His friend's strangely-coloured eyes had gone distant.

'They're back,' Husam breathed, the words barely more than a whisper.

A chill ran down Tembo's back. It was like looking at a physical echo of Kasau, the strange dragonhunter who had suffered an untimely death a week before. Kasau had led their now scattered party of hunters northwards through Racafi and half-way across Orupee in pursuit of two rare dragons.

The authorities restricted hunters to killing rogue dragons – those causing trouble to human communities. The hunting of dragons that had found their dragonriders was strictly forbidden, but Kasau had convinced their party that the potential riches to be gained from a successful hunt in this case outweighed any risks. Tembo felt it unlikely that Kasau had been motivated by wealth. He did not seem bothered by material possessions. The man had been unusual in many ways, not least in his possession of instincts unlike anything Tembo and Husam had ever seen before. Strangely, since Kasau's death, Husam was beginning to mirror those instincts and abilities.

There had been an unnatural edge to the slim dragonhunter these past few days. Ever since that fateful night attack on the dragons had resulted in Kasau's death, Husam had been different. It wasn't just the visible change in the colour of his eyes. His personality had changed as well. He was colder, and less impulsive.

Tembo had asked him about this, but Husam carefully avoided answering. He claimed he did not feel any different, but this was an open lie that both understood was his way of saying 'Don't ask me about it.' If Husam had not been such a good friend for the past two season rotations, Tembo would have left him and made his way home to Racafi. Whatever had happened to Husam the night Kasau died, it had affected his friend deeply.

There were times when Husam spoke and acted like his old self. During these moments it was as if nothing had happened, but those times were growing less frequent every day.

'What do you want to do?' Tembo asked cautiously.

'We're not ready to hunt them,' Husam replied thoughtfully, fingering Kasau's dragonbone spear. He had retrieved it from the meadow the day after the dragons had left, along with several dragonbone spear tips. 'We need more men. Some of the other hunters are still in the vicinity. It's time to begin gathering our own hunting party, Tembo.'

Tembo was relieved. He had wondered for a moment if Husam would announce some crazy plan for the two of them to try to kill the dawn dragon on their own. The dragon was far from being an easy target since it had teamed up with three other dragons. Aside from the dangers associated with illegally hunting a dragon that was partnered with a rider, the combination of powers possessed by the four dragons made for a formidable form of prey.

It was unusual for dragons to team up, particularly dragons of different types. Tembo had seen groups of up to three night dragons flying together and had once seen a pair of day dragons, but he had never heard of a day and a night dragon working together before. The two types of dragons and their riders were reputed to have been on the verge of war for centuries. Add to this the two less common dragon types – the dawn and dusk dragons – and this was by far the most unusual group of dragons he had ever come across.

'I'll go and start looking, Husam,' he said. 'How long do we have?'

'Not long this time,' the slim hunter replied, his eyes going distant again. 'But they'll be back, and next time they will separate. We'll get our chance, Tembo, but we've got a lot of work to do if we're to be ready.'

How *does* he know that? Once again Tembo was tempted to leave. He could walk away on the pretence of looking for other hunters and just keep walking, but he knew he would not do it. Despite all his misgivings, he felt a sense of responsibility towards his friend. They had watched one another's backs for a long time. He could not bring himself to abandon Husam now. His friend's behaviour was a mystery, but as with all such puzzles, there would be an answer.

My biggest problem, Tembo thought, is that, though I need an answer, I can't even decide on the question.

# Chapter Six
# 'They Are Fools.'

'You'd better land, Shadow. I'm not feeling too good.'

It was not an easy admission to make but, if Pell had learned anything from his recent experience, it was not to push past the boundaries of sense. He had been lucky once, and he must not push his luck. Having a dragon brought no guarantees of safety – very much the opposite. Flying was a dangerous business at the best of times.

Pride had forced him back into the saddle far earlier than was wise. He was still unsteady on his feet, his body ached all over and he had little strength in his arms and legs. However, the Great Quest to restore the Oracle was more important than a few aches and pains. He had told the others to expect him back with the orb within two weeks. Failure was not an option. Shadow had protested, but he could tell she was not wholehearted in her arguments. She wanted to press onwards as much as he did.

'I'm on my way down,' Shadow responded, instantly ceasing to beat her wings. They entered a shallow glide. 'Would you like me to find a village, or would you rather we camped out tonight?'

The thought of a bed was tempting, but Pell had given more than half of his money to the widow and her daughter. He had enough left to pay for a night of lodging in an inn, but not much more. And they did not have time to stop at a town to earn money.

He sighed, resigned to the idea of an uncomfortable night. 'We'd better camp,' he told her. 'See if you can find somewhere close to running water. I'll need to drink a lot for the next few days. My father taught me that drinking water was very good for speeding the recovery from injuries and my water carrier doesn't hold much.'

Shadow's head twisted from side to side as she scanned the countryside ahead for a suitable landing place. Dipping her wing a little to the left, she turned gently northwards a few degrees and continued her glide. Pell trusted Shadow implicitly. She was consistently successful at locating good places to stop.

The ground was getting closer. Pell guessed they

were about five hundred spans up – high enough that everything still felt unreal, but low enough to pick out a reasonable amount of detail on the ground below. The terrain looked flat from this height, but he knew from previous experience of this region that it was actually gently rolling. Villages were sparse, but the land was fertile and people who had settled here were mainly self-sufficient.

As they descended lower, more detail became clear. Where cows had been white and brown blobs in the fields before, now they clearly had legs and heads. At about the same time as he began to pick out legs on sheep, the animals on the ground started to become aware of Shadow. Herds of cattle and sheep scattered as they passed overhead, spooked by the danger posed by the presence of a top predator.

Pell sensed Shadow's pleasure in the response she commanded. She was not hungry enough to want to hunt yet, and she would not take a farm animal by choice. Shadow genuinely preferred to hunt those animals that roamed free. If given the choice, she was most likely to eat a deer or a wild goat. Deer were plentiful in eastern Orupee, so she would have no problem finding tasty food.

At about fifty spans above the ground, the

treetops suddenly seemed to leap upwards towards them. It felt as if they passed a strange transition point where the ground stopped being a multi-coloured carpet and sprang into three-dimensional reality. The final moments before they swept down to a gentle landing at the edge of a tree-lined stream brought the familiar rush of adrenalin to Pell's stomach.

In those final moments before touchdown everything appeared to accelerate and the surreal world of the air gave way to the hard reality of the earth. It was those few heartbeats as Shadow decelerated to a speed at which her legs could take over and run them to a gentle stop that always set Pell's heart racing. If she landed too fast, her legs would not be able to run fast enough and Shadow would nose-dive into the earth with potentially disastrous consequences. Slow down too much, and her wings would no longer create enough lift to keep them in the air, resulting in a rapid vertical drop. It was a fine line, but one that Shadow trod with apparent ease no matter how hard the wind tried to fool her.

The conditions today were benign, with a light breeze and a flat landing surface. Pell would have found it easy to relax and enjoy the final rush and running stop but for the pain throughout his body.

As they came to a halt, he groaned and immediately eased his right leg over to join his left so that he could slide gently down to the ground.

Reaching up, he grabbed the water carrier from where it was hooked onto the saddle. It was a hot afternoon down here at ground level. The sun was making its descent towards the horizon, but the ground was still radiating the heat it had soaked up during the afternoon and Pell felt sweat begin to trickle down his back from the moment he dismounted. He took a long swig from the carrier and replaced the stopper before shedding his jacket and over-trousers.

He squinted at the reddening sun. Dusk would not linger tonight. He did not have long to build any sort of shelter. Just the thought of work brought another groan to his lips.

*'Don't worry, Pell. I'll shelter you tonight. If I curl up into a circle, you can sleep in the middle under my wing. You can't have a fire there, but you should be warm enough. My body will provide sufficient heat.'*

'Thank you, Shadow,' he replied aloud. He leaned against her side and rested his cheek against her scales. *'Thank you so much.'*

It was unnecessary to say more. Shadow knew his thoughts. She could sense his feelings of love and gratitude. He stayed close for a few seconds before pushing himself upright and stumbling across to the stream to see what the water was like.

Walking was agony. Spikes of pain originated all up his back. His legs felt weak and the muscles in both his legs and arms burned as if he had overused them, though he had done little other than sit in the saddle.

He reached the stream. The water was shallow, fast running and clean. He took another swig from his water carrier and then knelt down next to the brook and laid it with the open neck into the flow. It filled quickly and he tasted from it again. The fresh water was cool and refreshing, but rather than making him feel more awake it pushed him closer towards sleep.

All of a sudden he began to feel dizzy. Jamming the stopper into the carrier, he staggered to his feet and took a few crazy steps back towards Shadow. The dragon blurred and the world spun out of control. He was falling, or was he? He could no longer tell.

He did not feel the impact of the ground. Nor did he notice his dragon approach and encircle him with her body. The sun dived below the horizon and dusk gave way to night. Shadow tried touching his mind with hers a few times, but he was totally unresponsive. If she had not been familiar with the feel of Pell's mind when he was in deep sleep, she might have panicked, but she could tell his unconscious state was due to exhaustion rather than as a result of his injuries. He pushed himself hard. She respected that, but she knew she would need to watch him closely, or risk losing him for ever.

'I didn't wait centuries to have you burn out in a few short seasons, Pell. Sleep,' she ordered him. 'Sleep well, dragonrider. The orb will wait a little longer.'

For the next few days Shadow flew faster than she had ever flown before. Not because she felt driven by the Oracle's quest, but because she knew it would minimise her rider's need to spend time in the saddle. With mighty sweeps of her great wings she drove them at a tremendous pace over Eastern Orupee, across the sea to Isaa and on towards the great mountain range that harboured the enclave of the night dragons. Pell was grateful for every rest stop that Shadow made. There was an unspoken understanding between them. The pace when they were airborne was furious, and even resting at night had a similarly intense air about it.

Day by day Pell's strength improved until he regained enough stamina to manage longer spells in the air. By the time they came within sight of the home range of the night dragons, he had lost all sense of time. They might have been travelling six days or sixty for all he could remember. The journey was a blur of mounting and dismounting, frantic flying and breathless rest stops.

Shadow was nearly as tired as he was. He could feel her fatigue through their bond. She had pushed herself to the limit. But the weather had been kind – the prevailing westerly wind had aided them all the way and they had gained back the entire day they had lost after his fall. So long as they secured the orb quickly and set a steady pace on the return journey, they should make it within the fortnight.

For the first time since he had left Elian and the others, Pell suddenly wondered what he would do if he could not find the orb. What if it was not at the enclave, but in some distant corner of the world? He shook off the thought. The dying Oracle had given them the rhyme to guide their path to the orbs:

*Release the dark orb – death brings me life.*
*Take brave ones' counsel, 'ware ye the knife.*
*Exercise caution, stay pure and heed,*
*Yield unto justice: truth will succeed.*

The meaning of his verse seemed clear. The 'dark orb' must be the orb of the night dragons. He was to seek the counsel of the 'brave ones'. Who could that be, if not the leaders of the night dragon enclave? He felt sure the verse did not refer to anyone from the day dragon enclave, no matter what the other riders had said. He was supposed to come here. He could feel it. He was following his destiny.

The mountains loomed ahead of them; purple-grey with majestic white caps. They were taller and altogether more imposing than the mountains of central Orupee. Excitement warred with nervousness within Pell's chest as they drew ever closer. Shadow turned slightly south towards the pass they would need to enter to reach the enclave.

*'The watch dragons have seen us,'* she announced.

*'Already?'* Pell said, more than a little surprised. *'But we're still leagues away!'*

*'They are ever vigilant. Segun would have them severely punished if they are found to not be so.'*

Ah, yes! Segun, he thought to himself. Self-styled, yet accepted, leader of the night dragon riders. Just the thought of him sent a shiver down Pell's spine that was half fear, half excitement. The man had a reputation for being both brilliant and ruthless. The senior riders were all loyal to him. He had long since ejected from the inner ring of power any who disagreed with his thinking. He was not a man to cross. Well I've no intention of annoying him, Pell thought. I'm here to impress . . . and to find the orb, of course.

Squinting upwards, he could just make out the watch dragons sitting on rocky outcrops high up on the shoulders of the mountains that towered into the sky on both sides of the pass. Quite why Segun felt it necessary to guard the passes into the range, Pell could not begin to imagine. There was no power in Areth strong enough to assault the stronghold of the night dragons, except maybe the entire enclave of day dragons – but that would never happen. The day dragons were too wound up in their sense of nobility to attempt a sneak attack. If they ever did challenge the night dragons, they would do so openly.

As Shadow drew parallel, the two dragons launched, stooping like giant falcons from above. Pell could sense Shadow's nonchalance through the bond, so he felt no real concern as the two dragons dived towards them in a coordinated mock attack.

'*Ignore them. They're just showing off,*' Shadow said, her tone derisive. '*They are fools. To attack like that for real would invite disaster. They have generated too much momentum to change their attack path now. A simple tight turn would throw their little game into chaos.*'

'*Do it then!*' Pell urged.

'*No. Don't react. Just keep looking forwards.*'

The two watch dragons whistled past them, each giving a bellowing roar as it dived with talons extended. Shadow continued to fly ahead, not deviating so much as a hair's-width from her chosen course. Pell did as he was told and kept his head and eyes straight ahead, though his stomach leaped at the sudden noise of the great dragon voices. He felt the disturbance of their passage in the air around him. The dragons had missed them by no more than a few spans.

'*Well done,*' Shadow said, pleased. '*Keep ignoring them. It's the best response to such nonsense.*'

'*But why didn't you make fools of them?*' Pell asked, gritting his teeth with frustration at having to let these dragonriders literally fly rings around them. Both watch dragons had now zoomed back to position themselves on either side of Shadow.

'*Because I did not wish to be responsible for the unnecessary deaths of my fellow night dragons and their riders,*' Shadow responded. '*What they just did was both ridiculous and very dangerous. One wrong move by either could have seen them crash into each other. At that speed and height a collision could have proved fatal for both the dragons and their riders. Don't worry. I imagine Segun and his dragon, Widewing, will be as unimpressed with their idiotic behaviour as I am. They do not suffer fools gladly.'*

Shadow was right, Pell realised. But knowing this did not make ignoring the two watch riders any easier. His competitive spirit yearned to demonstrate that he and Shadow were more than a match for them. If he had not been under time pressure to present his request to Segun, he might have pushed Shadow into showing the two watch dragons and their riders some real flying skill. But the meeting with Segun was far more important. When Segun and his council of senior riders discovered that Pell and Shadow were here as part of the Great Quest, everything would change. His status would rise. If he succeeded in the Quest, he might even be invited to join the senior council.

Pell quashed any thoughts about reacting to the watch riders and kept his focus forwards. The watch dragons flanked them for a while, but soon lost interest and turned back to retake their places on the watch posts.

Shadow powered up the pass and into the maze of mountains beyond. It was well that she knew the range intimately, for Pell realised it would be easy to get lost amongst the peaks. He had not come here often during the two season rotations since he and Shadow had met, but his previous visits had failed to give him any sense of familiarity with the route through the valleys.

It was theoretically possible to enter the mountains at any point, but there were only three main routes into the heart of the range that did not require risking the dangerously thin air of high altitude flying. Dragons could enter over the peaks, but it was not without risk, and several foolhardy riders had died attempting it. This made the night dragon enclave the most difficult of the four enclaves to access, but the easiest to defend.

They dropped down the other side of the pass into a great valley that ran northwest to southeast, and Shadow made a gentle turn to the right. The sheer scale of his surroundings made Pell feel very small and fragile, and for a moment he understood what it might feel like to be a fly weaving through a crowd of humans armed with swatters. This vulnerability did not generate fear, rather an edginess that heightened his awareness.

Flying in the vicinity of such huge mountains was never without danger. Even in fair weather there were numerous traps for the unwary. Valleys funnelled wind, accelerating the air and creating swirling eddies in the most unexpected places. Then there were vicious up- and down-drafts that could be caused by any number of triggers. Under certain conditions, the air crossing the mountains could even react in such a way that severe air currents, like great waves, could be experienced up to one hundred leagues away. As they turned up that first major valley, Pell wound safety straps around his wrists and checked that his feet were securely fixed in the stirrups.

The next hour was a medley of bumps and stomach-lurching drops as Shadow navigated through the valleys and inner passes. The final, tight V-shaped valley was particularly treacherous. Air currents swirled, whistling around the craggy cliff walls and howling over hollows with the voice of an invisible giant.

As they rounded the final bend he saw the most unforgettable view in this mountain range. The valley widened out into a bowl-shaped dead end. The sheer cliff at the end was riddled with caves. Many were natural in origin, though many more had been carved out to make new habitations for the numerous night dragons. This was the home of the enclave.

Black dragons perched on ledges and rocky outcrops. The vast grey wall looked as if a swarm of giant rock-worms had made their homes there. So many great black openings dotted the face of the cliff that Pell wondered again why the mountainside had not collapsed.

Pell's heart began to accelerate as Shadow proceeded without hesitation to one of the largest caves, high up the mountainside.

This is it, Pell thought, unable to contain his excitement as they approached the gaping maw of the cave. Our time is here at last.

## Chapter Seven
# Segun

'The Great Quest, you say?' the rider asked. 'Yes, Segun will want to see you immediately. Come. Follow me and I'll lead you to him. What was your name again?'

'Pell. Rider of Whispering Shadow,' Pell replied, keeping his voice calm and steady.

The rider's response was exactly as Pell had imagined. The hint of excitement in the man's voice, the urgency with which he was taking Pell to meet Segun – everything was exactly as it should be. So why did he suddenly have a bad feeling brewing in his stomach?

*'What's the matter, Pell? Is everything all right?'*

'Yes. Everything's fine, *Shadow,*' he replied. *'I'm probably just a bit nervous about meeting Segun.'*

*'You'll be fine, Pell. You're my rider. Together we*

make as formidable a partnership as any in the night dragon enclave. You have nothing to fear. Be strong. I'm told Segun respects strength.'

'Normally that wouldn't be a problem, but it's hard to imagine being strong when I'm still sore from my fall.'

'You have recovered quickly,' Shadow responded without pause. 'Many would have taken weeks before riding again after such injuries. You were on my back the next day. You are strong, Pell. Do not forget that in Segun's presence. I am being ushered out of the cave-mouth now. I shall have the honour of sitting with Widewing and the other senior dragons while you meet with Segun, but I'll be out of range of your thoughts. Good luck, dragonrider. Do not fear. We will find success together. I feel it.'

Shadow's words were warming, but Pell could not totally shake the uneasy feeling in the pit of his stomach. By the time he reached the solid wooden door set into a small stone archway in the right-hand wall of the cave, he realised that any second thoughts were irrelevant now. He had come too far to turn back.

The rider opened the door and led the way through. Pell had to stoop under the arch. On the other side was a tunnel, lit by a line of torches that were visible for some distance. The walls were rough and unfinished, the subterranean corridor hewn into a functional walkway. Thick wooden supports shored up the roof at regular intervals, setting Pell to wondering about the stability of the caves. The more his mind questioned, the more he imagined the weight of the mountain pressing down above him. If the roof collapsed, he would be squashed flat in a heartbeat. The knowledge made him feel tiny and fragile, like a bug. It was not a pleasant sensation.

Although Pell could walk upright along the passageway, he had to duck under the support stays to avoid hitting his head on the crossbeams. They passed several doors along the passageway, but his guide did not so much as glance at them. When they rounded the bend, the end of the corridor became apparent. The door at the far end was no different from the others, save for an image of a black night dragon, forged from metal and inset into the wood.

The rider rapped hard on the door with his knuckles and then opened it without waiting for a response.

'What is it, Murvan? I told you we were not to be disturbed.'

The voice was hard as granite, and almost as rough.

'A rider named Pell wishes an audience, my Lord. Claims he's here on the Great Quest.'

There was a brief silence, followed by some rapid, excited muttering that Pell could not make out. 'My Lord?' he thought. He called Segun 'my Lord', but nobility's *never* been recognised amongst dragonriders! Besides, Segun came from a humble farming family. There's something strange going on here.

'Show him in then, Murvan. And prepare quarters and escorts for him as we discussed.'

The voice, now commanding, held no apology. Segun, it appeared, felt himself above the need for politeness. It was also clear that Pell was expected. That was something of a surprise. How had they known he was coming?

Pell was ushered forwards through the door and into the chamber beyond. The interior was as intimidating as Segun's voice: hard lines, bleak furnishing and a huge, stylised night dragon motif, black as the dead of night, adorning each wall.

A large rectangular table dominated the centre of the chamber. Six men sat at the table, but there was no mistaking Segun. There was an undeniable aura of charisma and leadership about him. Even seated, Pell could tell he was taller than average. His face was clean-shaven, with strong features and a noticeable cleft in his chin. Dark hair, cropped short, showed hints of grey at the temples, but all of these details were incidental compared to his eyes. Segun possessed pale blue eyes, the like of which Pell had never seen before. Shadowed by heavy black brows, they burned out of Segun's head with the icy power of a glacier.

'Welcome, Pell, rider of . . .'

'Whispering Shadow,' Pell provided, deliberately not adding 'my Lord', but unsure exactly how to address Segun.

'Of course,' Segun replied, his voice suddenly much smoother. 'From the Steppes of Central Isaa. You met with Shadow around two season rotations ago if memory serves.'

'That's right.'

'Good. So what can I do for you, Pell? You claim you're here on the Great Quest.' Segun stared unblinking at Pell as he waited for a response.

It was unnerving to be the focus of such intense concentration. Pell's mouth went dry and he ran his tongue around the inside of his lips, searching for moisture as his tongue started to swell. The other five riders around the table were all watching him with nearly as much fervour as Segun. If he was ever going to join them he knew he had to put in the performance of his life.

'That's right,' Pell replied slowly. 'I've come to ask your help – the help of you all. I need to find the night dragon orb. The Oracle gave us cryptic instructions. Those referring to the night dragon orb have led me here to you.'

'"Gave *us* instructions"? Of course, there are always others involved in the Great Quest,' Segun said thoughtfully, glancing around pointedly at his inner council of riders. 'Please, tell us more. We have been aware for some time that the Oracle's strength is failing. Despite this, it's been a long time since anyone attempted the Great Quest. You must be an exceptional group of riders to be given such a huge responsibility. The Oracle clearly thinks very highly of you to place its existence in your hands.'

Pell's chest swelled with pride at the compliments. All doubts and misgivings about this meeting melted in that instant. He felt the tension drain from his muscles and he began, hesitantly at first, but then with growing confidence, to tell them about his quest.

First he told what he knew of the other riders, his first impressions of each of their characters and what little he knew of their backgrounds. The encounter with the Oracle he described in great detail, but then he skimmed through the battle with the dragonhunters and his decision to pursue the night dragon orb alone, rather than risk unnecessary conflict by going with the others to the day dragon enclave. Day and night dragons had teetered on the brink of open conflict for centuries. Only the influence of the Oracle had prevented what many felt was an inevitable confrontation. Pell felt confident that his decision would not be interpreted as cowardice but as a sensible precaution to avoid becoming a catalyst for full-scale war. He said nothing about his fall, but gave a detailed account of the antics of the watch dragons at the Eastern Pass.

Segun and his inner council sat in silence throughout his account, listening most attentively to every word. When he finished, he was gratified to see Segun lean close to those on either side of him and he watched as they whispered back and forth with serious faces. The importance of his mission was not lost on them.

'As I said at the beginning, I'm here to ask your aid,' Pell added after a moment. 'Can you help me find the night dragon orb?'

Segun turned to face him, clearly irritated at the interruption to his whispered conference, but holding his anger in check. For a moment, Pell felt as strong and powerful as Shadow had told him he was.

'Tell me the rhyme again. The one you say relates to the night dragon orb,' Segun ordered.

'Very well,' Pell replied, slightly taken aback by the underlying aggression in Segun's voice. *'Release the dark orb – death brings me life. Take brave ones' counsel, 'ware ye the knife. Exercise caution, stay pure and heed, Yield unto justice: truth will succeed.'*

Segun looked around at the other riders. Each nodded as Segun looked at them.

'And you're sure there's nothing else you can tell me about your quest, or the other riders?' the night dragon leader asked, his piercing eyes probing Pell's once more.

'I'm sure. I've told you everything I know.'

'Then I must thank you, Pell. You have done the Night Dragon Council a great service by bringing this information to us today. We've long held that the Oracle's power over dragonkind has become an unnecessary burden. Now you've presented us with the perfect opportunity to rid the world of its influence for good. The Oracle's demise will finally allow dragons and their riders to assume their natural place in society – at its head.'

'But ... I don't understand,' Pell spluttered. 'Without the Oracle dragonkind will die.'

'No!' Segun snapped, his pale eyes flashing with uncontrolled anger now. 'That's what the Oracle would have us believe. Why that meddling spirit has denied us our rightful place in society has been a mystery for centuries. The Oracle has had the dragons under its spell for too long. They are blinded by their loyalty to it. The truth is, dragonkind will expand and flourish without the Oracle. Dragonkind will rise to dominate the world. No more dragon hunts. No more disrespect. None will dare stand against us. You must end your quest for the orb. The Great Quest must not be completed, or dragonkind will be tied to further millennia of servitude.'

Segun's anger and intensity was intimidating, but despite the aura of power he emanated, Pell felt the fire of anger responding in his own belly. Of all the night dragon riders who could have been chosen for the Great Quest, the Oracle had found him worthy. Not Segun, nor any of his cronies, but Pell, rider of Whispering Shadow. It was his moment of glory and he was not about to give it up without a fight.

'But what if you're wrong?' Pell asked through gritted teeth. 'What then?'

One of Segun's lieutenants sucked a sharp intake of breath between his teeth and Segun's eyes widened with surprise before narrowing into thin slits that spat fury. There was a scrape of wood on stone as some of the men began to get to their feet, and a flash of steel sent Pell's mind reeling. *'Ware ye the knife . . . 'ware ye the knife . . .* The words of the Oracle's verse echoed. As his eyes flicked to the knife that had appeared in the man's hand, he flinched.

Segun's hand signal to his men commanded an instant response. The knife vanished back into its sheath and the men sank back to their seats. Pell's heart was racing as he carefully let out the deep breath he had instinctively drawn. Rather than shrink away from Segun's potential wrath, Pell drew himself to his full height and looked him straight in the eye.

'I am not wrong,' Segun said softly, his voice beginning as barely more than a whisper, but rising rapidly. 'Who do you think you are, Pell? You are nobody. Nobody! And you will remain nobody unless I decide to make you somebody. The Oracle has outlived its time. It must be allowed to die. Will you defy my will?'

'It seems that somebody must,' Pell answered, setting his chin forwards at a defiant angle. 'I was chosen. It's my destiny to find the orb. I can feel it. Though it saddens me to admit it, my companions were right – you cannot be the "brave ones" I seek. I shall direct my efforts elsewhere.'

He turned to leave.

'Murvan!' Segun's command was loud and gained an instant response. The door flung open and six burly men marched in to block Pell's exit. He turned back to face Segun, who was now the only person still seated. His lieutenants were already in motion around the table. Pell was surrounded.

He knew better than to try to fight his way out. He was big for his age, but still tender from his fall and there were a dozen fully-grown men here.

'So what are you going to do now, Segun?' Pell snapped. 'Have me killed and my dragon will go berserk. You don't want to see what she's capable of when she's angry.'

Segun smiled, but there was more cruelty than mirth in the expression. 'I have no need to kill you, Pell,' he said. 'You're not worthy of the attention that death would bring you. Don't worry. You'll be released soon enough. Right after we destroy the night orb. Maybe then you'll see sense and take your place amongst our ranks as we ride to forge a new order across Areth. Take him to a holding cell, Murvan.'

'Yes, my Lord.'

'You won't get away with this, Segun,' Pell warned.

'That's *Lord* Segun to you, boy. And believe me

when I say that I will get away with whatever I wish. The Age of Dragons is coming, and I will be its architect.'

## Chapter Eight

# Warm Stones and a Fresh Start

As Nolita took the orb from the saddlebag, the light level in the chamber brightened slightly. The orb felt almost greasy in her hands and she shuddered at the sensation. All attention was on the great chasm. A sigh like the breath of a dragon preceded the arrival of the Oracle. The misty being surged from the depths in a swirl of smoke-like vapour that twisted and twirled in a mesmerising pattern before resolving into the great dragon's head-shape they had seen during their last encounter.

'*Ah! The Orb of Blood!*' The Oracle's voice rang in the minds of the riders like a giant bell. '*I knew ye would not fail me, Nolita. Well done. Well done indeed! Come. Cast it into my well.*'

Nolita stepped forwards with the crystal globe cradled in her hands. Although she knew it was irrational, especially as she disliked handling it, she felt suddenly reluctant to part with it. Thoughts of what she had endured to gain it flashed through her mind: the terrors of the Chamber of the Sun's Steps, the horror as the orb sucked the blood from her fingers, and the dangers posed by the giant snake and the ravening pack of dogs. The orb was a liability, but despite this it felt strangely precious. It represented an achievement greater than anything she had ever dreamed possible – the conquering of her deepest fears. A moment ago she would have been glad to hurl it into the black depths of the great pit, but now . . .

It took all her resolve, but Nolita stepped slowly forwards to the edge of the well. The figure of the Oracle towered above her.

'Go on, Nolita,' Elian urged, mistaking her reluctance for fright. 'There's nothing to be afraid of here. The Oracle needs the orb. Throw it in. Get rid of it and we can move on. We've still got three more to find.'

'*Do it, Nolita. Be free,*' Firestorm added in the secrecy of her mind.

Nolita closed her eyes. She stood at the edge of the great well, but she felt no fear. Her heart felt free from its grip for the first time in a long while. If there was anywhere in Areth that she felt totally safe, it was here in the presence of the Oracle. So why was she hesitating? Taking a deep breath, she drew the orb momentarily to her chest and then pushed it away from her, opening her fingers to release it. There was no sound of its passage into the depths. No distant crash of smashing crystal. Nothing. She opened her eyes, half expecting to see the orb miraculously suspended in midair, but it was gone.

'Ahhh!' sighed the Oracle. '*The first part of the quest is complete, but time is against ye and there is still far to go. Pell has strayed from the path, making your journey ahead both longer and more perilous. He has followed his heart, rather than my words. Do ye know where he has gone?*'

It was Elian who answered. 'To the enclave of the night dragons,' he said. 'He should have sought out the griffins. We learned this from Barnabas, but Pell misinterpreted your riddle.'

'*Indeed he did,*' the Oracle intoned. '*And also ignored my direction to work together. Now we may all pay the price for his misjudgement, for he will alert Segun to the quest. The night dragon leader would have ye fail, and see me pass away for ever. He and his followers will look to stop ye by any means they can. They think to free dragons from the life purpose I bring, but they do not understand its importance. Without*

100

*purpose, dragonkind will descend into anarchy. All that dragons have achieved in Areth will wither and fade to dust. There was a time when each dragon type looked to one of my race for guidance. Now I am the last of my kind. Agree with me or not, dragons no longer have a choice if they are to survive. The burden lays heavily on me, but I urge ye – complete the task without delay.'*

Nolita shivered. Her part was done, but she was still trapped. There was no option for her to stand aside and let the others continue without her. In truth, whilst the thought of more dangerous journeying chilled her, the idea of being left behind with Firestorm was worse. Mastering her fear was one thing, but she had come to rely heavily on Elian and Kira for support and encouragement. To face her fear of Firestorm without their company was unthinkable.

'What will Segun do?' asked Kira.

*'I believe he will attempt to reach one of the orbs before ye and destroy it,'* the Oracle replied. *'If his efforts fail, however, beware. Segun is ruthless, and his inner circle follows him with unthinking loyalty. He will not hesitate to have ye killed if he feels it necessary.'*

'So we should go straight to the griffins and get the night orb before Segun has a chance,' Kira said, looking around at Elian and Nolita for confirmation.

Elian met her eyes and gave a quick nod of support.

Nolita, however, remained staring at the Oracle. 'No,' she said slowly. 'That road is not open to us.'

'What!' Kira exclaimed. 'Why not?'

'*Nolita is correct,*' the Oracle confirmed. '*Ye must find Pell before ye continue the quest. Only the appropriate dragon and rider can retrieve each orb. Without Pell ye will fail.*'

Kira muttered something unintelligible under her breath, though Nolita did not need to hear it to know the language was not polite.

'Then we're going to have to visit the enclave of the night dragons,' Elian said thoughtfully. 'Shadow is fast. Pell could be there by now, but if we go through the gateways, we won't be far behind. I believe it's safe to assume that Pell won't be subtle with his enquiries. He'll go straight to Segun. Let's assume the night dragon leader will understand the riddle enough to recognise "the brave ones" as the griffins. Given what the Oracle has told us about him, what do you think Segun will do with Pell, Kira?'

Kira thought for a moment. 'Lock him up,' she said. 'It's the obvious solution. Fang agrees with me. He thinks Segun will have Pell confined somewhere that Shadow can't reach him, and then go after the orb himself.'

'*Thou speakest sound logic, Kira,*' the Oracle confirmed. '*It is as I have foreseen. Ye must go. Time is as much your enemy as any other. Ye must rescue Pell and attain the night orb before Segun can destroy it. Good luck.*'

With this there was another breathy sigh. Dragons and riders alike watched with fascination as the misty apparition folded inwards, sinking back into the unfathomable black depths of the circular chasm. The light in the cavern dimmed slightly with its departure, leaving them all momentarily entranced and staring at the great well.

Kira was first to snap out of it. 'Come on. Let's get going,' she said.

Nolita could not help but admire her. She wished she could find Kira's strength and courage. Life would then be very different. The dusk dragon rider strode off up the ramp towards the mouth of the cave. There was an air of determination surrounding her. Elian turned to Nolita and waited for her to join him before stepping out to follow Kira. Nolita gave him a smile. He was so polite. She was sure he imagined himself as a knight of the air. There was a naïve nobility about the way he approached everything. She found it rather sweet, but knew he would need to grow up fast if they encountered Segun and his henchmen. Rumour had it that the night dragon riders did not stand on ceremony. They stopped at nothing to meet their aims. A sense of honour was fine, she concluded . . . up to a point.

When they reached the mouth of the cave, the mist outside seemed thicker than before.

'*Do not worry, Nolita,*' Firestorm said, his voice inside her mind startling her. '*I can lead the way safely to the campsite we used after our last visit here. The flight will not take long.*'

She did not answer. Any flight, no matter how short, was traumatic. Every time she got airborne there seemed to be new dangers to face, or think about, to say nothing of the inner battle she had to fight with her fear to climb into the saddle in the first place. Despite the Oracle's words of praise for her success, and the pleasure they had brought, she still felt like an onion in a fruit bowl.

Nolita knew that even in fine weather they could not fly far or fast enough to find Pell and win the race to the night orb without using Aurora's gateways. A shudder rippled down her spine. The thought of visiting the strange world on the other side of the gateway again was not a pleasant one, but there appeared little choice.

'Come, Nolita. It's time we went. The others are ready.'

Firestorm was right. Her fellow riders were already mounted. She closed her eyes, gritted her teeth and sucked in a deep breath.

'There's no way out of here other than on a dragon's back,' she muttered to herself. 'It's the best reason you're ever going to have to climb into the saddle, so get on with it.'

The intimate shock of contact with Firestorm's scales as she scrambled up his side was as disturbing as ever. Nolita had thought it would dim with time, but the experience seemed as intense now as it did that first occasion in the Chamber of the Sun's Steps. Tears hovered in the corners of her eyes as she settled into the saddle and slotted her feet into the stirrups. Would it always be this difficult? she wondered.

Firestorm waited until he was sure Nolita was ready and then he ran forwards and launched off the ledge into the milky white air. As he had promised, the flight was short. The other two dragons stayed in close formation, one on either side until they descended to the familiar meadow by the wood.

As they dropped the final few spans, visibility improved and Nolita felt as if they were falling from a dream into the real world. To her surprise, she found she was soaked as she dismounted. She had not felt rain within the misty air, but moisture had seeped through her jacket, leaving her feeling cold and clammy.

Kira organised the rebuilding of their campsite with businesslike efficiency. Nolita found it hard to motivate herself to begin with, but the realisation that the sooner she completed her tasks, the sooner she could sit by the fire and dry out, provided the necessary mental nudge. Kira insisted on adding enough layers to the roofing of the shelter to ensure that it was unlikely to leak on them in the night. Nolita refilled all the water bottles, and then worked with Elian to find enough firewood to see them through the night.

Before long, they were all sitting around the fire, drying their boots and jackets. Kira lashed branches together with twine and made a makeshift clothes-horse on which they draped their soaking jackets. She had also sent Elian to fetch three large round stones from the stream to warm next to the fire.

'The stones will hold the heat of the fire for a long time,' she explained. 'If we wrap our spare tunics around them and place them at the bottom of the shelter when we go to bed, they should keep our feet warm tonight. It's a trick one of the hunters in my tribe taught me for staying comfortable when it's damp and cold.'

That night was the most comfortable Nolita had ever spent outside of a proper bed. When Elian woke her just before dawn it was raining and miserable, but she felt surprisingly positive. It was amazing what a difference having warm feet made to her night's sleep.

The shelter had not leaked, so they awoke dry and warm. Nolita felt so good when she woke up that she crawled over to Kira and gave her a hug. Kira looked embarrassed, but pleased.

'I'd hug you as well if I wasn't worried about that knife of yours,' Elian told Kira, giving a cheeky wink from the other side of the shelter. 'Those warm stones were a great idea. I think I'll start doing that every night, whether I'm camping or not.'

'I wonder what an innkeeper would think of that,' Kira said, clearly amused by the notion. 'Come on. We'd better grab something to eat before we go through the gateway. There's no telling what time it will be on the other side, or whether we'll get a chance to eat while we're there.'

'At least we won't have to worry about being chased by dogs now we've got rid of the orb,' Elian said thankfully.

'True,' she replied. 'But that other world's so full

of danger there's no telling what'll happen. It feels like we're starting the quest all over again, and I suppose we are in a way. Here – let's make it a fresh start on a full stomach. Have some bread and cheese. There's not long until dawn.'

Pell was seething. He crouched next to the door and peered through the keyhole. It had taken a while to calm down from his initial fury. His hands hurt from where he had pounded the door of the cell with his fists, and his throat was sore from yelling at the guards who had dragged him here. His rage had passed, but now his mind went over and over his options. He did not have many.

There was not much to see through the little hole. The passageway outside was lit, but his field of vision was severely limited. He could hear men talking quietly outside the door. 'Guards probably,' he realised. 'But what makes them think they need to guard this door? It's so solid there's no chance of my breaking through it.'

They had not left him a light within the cell, but after a time his eyes had adjusted to what little seeped under the door and through the keyhole. The room was tiny – about two paces square, with nothing inside but a low cot with a rough rush mattress on one side and a small hole in the floor on the other. Given the stench emanating from the hole, it was clear this was his toilet facility. The smell made him want to vomit. What are the night dragon riders thinking of? he wondered. I don't get it. Why have they got such a disgusting little cell in the enclave? Surely Segun doesn't lock riders up regularly for having quests he disapproves of?

His best chance of escape was to get word to Shadow. He had tried calling to her, but she was not answering. She must be too far away, he thought. But how long will it be before she realises something's wrong?

Even if Shadow did work out that Pell was in trouble, what could she do? There was no way for a dragon to get here. The passageway was too small, and he was being held deep within the rock. His only hope was to get to her.

There were two potential avenues of escape. The first involved fooling the guards, or overpowering them – neither of which seemed likely. The second was for someone on the outside to come and rescue him.

'Fat chance of that!' he muttered. 'The others are two continents away trying to coax a shred of bravery out of Nolita.'

For a moment he wondered how they were doing. The idea that Nolita might succeed in obtaining an orb while he faced failure did not bear thinking about. A sick feeling settled in the pit of his stomach.

No, he thought. Don't even go there! Segun be damned! I'll not give up so easily. There has to be a way out of here. There has to. It's just a matter of finding it.

## Chapter Nine
# Like a Dark Angel

'Is it dusk, or nearly dawn, Ra?' Elian asked as he shook off the effects of the twisting wrench of emergence into the other world.

'Nearly dawn,' she answered immediately. 'But I'm not sure whether that's good, or bad.'

'It's a good thing, isn't it?' Elian said, confused by her response. 'The less time we spend in this world, the better.'

'You are right, Elian,' Aurora said, her tone sounding tired. 'But it means I have to make another gateway very soon and I will hardly have had time to recover from forming this one. You know how tiring it is. I'm sure you can feel it through the bond by now.'

He could. Aurora's fatigue was not as deep as it had been during their recent journey to Racafi, but she was always tired immediately after forming a gateway. It was clear that there was an optimum time between jumps that allowed her a full recovery. Unless they waited another whole day for her to get her inner strength back, she would have to draw deep on her reserves to get them back to Areth.

'Will you be all right?' He asked the question, but he instinctively knew her answer before she replied.

'Yes, Elian. I'll be fine. I'll be tired again for a while, but I will recover. I'm just not used to this. I've already formed more gateways since meeting you than I have in the rest of my life.' She paused a moment then said, 'That's strange! It's him again.'

'Him? Who?' Elian asked. 'The man in the flying machine, you mean? Where?'

'Below us,' she answered. 'It looks as if he's going to land. He's nervous. I sense that what he's about to do is very dangerous. Ah! It appears we have emerged further east than before. We are deep into territory belonging to the man's adversaries.'

'Then what in Areth does he think he's doing landing here?' Elian exclaimed aloud. 'Is he trying to get himself killed?'

'On the contrary, Elian,' Aurora replied. 'He's trying to save a compatriot. I can dimly sense his thoughts. He is here to recover one of his own people, but he's flying into a trap.'

'A trap? What sort of trap?'

'There are many men hidden in the bushes along the edge of the field he is descending towards. They are waiting for him.'

Elian leaned first to his left and then his right, trying to see the area Aurora was talking about. He could just about make out the flying machine below them, circling a large field. The field had a thick hedge around it, studded with many large trees. The light was too poor to see more detail.

'There is a man standing in the field waving to our flying friend, deliberately drawing him down, but he is also an enemy. I can sense the man he is looking for. He is scared and hiding in a ditch some distance away.'

Elian's mind raced. The same man again. They had seen him during both their first visit to this world, and again during their second, when he had aided them against a group of hostile flying machines. This had gone way beyond coincidence. The man's destiny *must* be tied with theirs, or why did they keep emerging near him? Unless they talked to him, they were unlikely to ever discover the reason. They could not let him be killed by this trap. The problem was: if they intervened this time, they would be seen by lots of people. What should they do?

*

Special Ops – the mission title covered a multitude of possibilities, but for Jack this had to be the worst. Picking up a member of the Secret Service from deep within enemy territory was fraught with danger. Just getting to the rendezvous required flying across enemy lines with no cover, navigating in the dark to a specific point, coping with ground fire and the possibility of enemy fighters without the benefit of a gunner in the front seat. Assuming he overcame these obstacles, and that the spy actually made it to the rendezvous point, there were a whole string of new problems to overcome to get home safely again. It was hardly a plum job.

Jack never liked getting up early, and missions didn't get much earlier than this. Getting into the cockpit feeling grumpy was never a recipe for success, but he had done his best to shake off his bad mood.

The particularly fierce anti-aircraft fire as he crossed the lines earlier had helped him regain his focus. Why pilots had nicknamed anti-aircraft fire 'Archie' was beyond him. He supposed it was easier for some to face their fear by laughing at it. By giving something so terrifying a friendly name, it made talking about it easier. Flying through Archie was never fun, but today the gunners seemed to have homed in on him much more quickly than usual. Explosions rocked his aircraft with alarming proximity. Some small shrapnel holes appeared in the wings, but nothing serious enough to worry Jack unduly.

As per the briefing, he found and followed the narrow grey road eastwards until it split. The expected railway line was visible to the right and the two small villages to his left. He followed the left fork of the road and tracked it until he reached a point where he was directly between two villages – one visible beyond each wingtip. The field to the left of the road was the pick-up point. This was the place. In the dim light it seemed the right shape.

Looking down he spotted a figure waving enthusiastically. Jack felt his heart begin to race. On his previous two such missions his contact had failed to show up. He had never been told why, but he could guess. The reason was not pretty. Spies were shown no mercy, and he knew that if he were caught retrieving this one, he would share the same fate.

These undercover guys are either incredibly brave or totally without sense, he thought. Suddenly another movement caught his eye. An enemy patrol was closing in on the spy's position. Jack could see the soldiers a couple of fields away, and more were moving along the road. If he was going to make the pick-up, he would have to be quick. He scanned the field again. There was no time for a thorough sweep. The enemy often set traps in known pick-up points. They dug trenches in the middle of fields and camouflaged them so that aircraft crashed into them on landing, or they strung wires across fields with similar results. He would have to risk it. There was no time for a close fly-by. With gritted teeth, he dipped the nose of the twin-seat FE2b into a descending turn.

'Let's get as close as we can, Jack my boy,' he muttered to himself. 'No point in making him run any further than he has to.'

The engine spluttered and popped at idle as he glided around the turn. He gave it a little burst of power as he levelled the wings, just to make sure it would respond. The throaty roar it gave as he momentarily pushed forwards the throttle was heart-warming, but it put him a little above the ideal approach path.

'A touch of side-slip,' he muttered, dipping the left wing and increasing his rate of descent by kicking the rudder to the right. 'Perfect!' He uncrossed the controls as he regained the perfect approach angle and eased the aircraft down until he was all but skimming the grass. Gently easing up the nose he allowed the wheels to gradually sink onto the surface with barely the whisper of a kiss. It was one of the best landings he had done in a while.

The surface was bumpy, but not terribly so. He trundled towards the waiting man, decelerating all the way. The shadowy figure had his hands up, as was the friendly protocol, but as Jack approached all hell broke loose. The spy took a spectacular dive to the ground even as the shadow of another figure seemed to fly down and hover next to him, hanging in the sky above him like a dark angel. At that same moment a barrage of rifle fire opened up from the hedgerow beyond.

'Bloody hell!' Jack swore. 'Come on! Get up! Get up! Over here – quickly!'

The man did not move. Either he was dead, injured, or he was too scared to move. It took a moment for Jack to realise that despite the sound and multiple flashes of gunfire, the air was not full of bullets. Either the enemy are lousy shots, or they're not shooting at me, he thought. As it turned out, neither assumption was correct. The hovering figure suddenly leaped down to earth and ran towards him. It took a moment for him to realise that it was a girl.

'What the . . .'

'Get ready to go!' she yelled. 'The man on the ground is not the person you're looking for. My friend has found your ally and is bringing him for you now. He was hiding not far from here. That man back there is your enemy,' she added, pointing to the man sprawled on the ground behind her.

Her accent was strange, but she spoke in English. Despite understanding her warning, Jack could make little sense of what was going on. A sudden whoosh of air drew his attention upwards. A great golden dragon swooped out of the dark blue sky and dropped a man onto the grass next to his aircraft. The man rolled over a couple of times and then sprang to his feet. He looked around, wild-eyed and poised to run. The dragon and rider did not stop. They powered back up into the pre-dawn sky.

It's the flying creatures! Jack thought, unwilling to label the creature with its proper name, as he was not sure he really believed his eyes. They're here again. But why? And where do they come from that they can appear so suddenly?

Whatever the girl had flown down on was completely invisible, yet the one that had dropped the spy showed no sign of disappearing. The horizon to the east was growing pale. Dawn was approaching fast. There was no time for specula-tion. He needed to get airborne and back across into friendly territory before the enemy fighters launched in force.

'Follow me back to my base,' Jack called out to the girl. 'I want to talk with you – thank you for your help. Do you understand me?'

'We can't,' she answered, looking anxiously eastwards towards the approaching dawn. 'There's no time. Take your friend and go! Go! Hurry! My dragon is taking a lot of hits from those foul weapons to shield you.'

So they *are* dragons, Jack thought. I'm not going mad.

The girl turned and leaped up into the air where she seemed to stick to and climb what appeared to be some sort of invisible staircase. A blast of fire lit the sky over the hedgerow where the enemy were concealed and another dragon swooped past. The fire from the dragon did not touch the hedgerow, but the rifle fire died to a brief shocked silence before resuming, this time directed at the departing dragon.

'GO!' she repeated over her shoulder again, anger lending her voice extra volume.

'You heard the girl!' Jack yelled at the spy, who was now staring with open-mouthed amazement at the departing silhouette. 'Come on, man! Get in! Don't ask questions. I've got no answers.'

The man scrambled into the front cockpit and began fumbling with the belts. Jack didn't wait.

He rammed the throttle forwards and began his take-off run. To his surprise the girl, now lying horizontal and still hanging in midair, matched his speed across the field next to him. He could see her out of the corner of his eye, maintaining position between him and the flashing muzzles of the enemy weapons. There was something else too. A sort of blurring under her body that nagged at his peripheral vision.

Jack knew better than to get distracted during a take-off run. Flying machines had a nasty habit of killing those who did not maintain their focus. He could no longer hear the reports of the enemy rifles above the roar of his engine, but he did not doubt he was still under fire. A sudden flare of dazzling bright light from behind him took Jack totally by surprise. It was like nothing he had ever experienced before. No man-made flare was that bright. For a moment it illuminated the countryside around his aircraft more clearly than full daylight and then it was gone, leaving him very glad that he had been facing away from the source. Even looking away from it there were after-effects. Greeny-yellow reflection spots danced before his eyes, making it difficult to see his instruments.

'Just concentrate on flying west,' he told himself. 'You won't go far wrong doing that.'

The seconds ticked by as he continued to climb. He squinted at the altimeter – four hundred feet and rising. The airspeed was stable. He was safely away from the ground. He looked down to his left and could see the road he had followed on his way into enemy territory snaking away to the south of his current course. He eased the aircraft left a few degrees to follow it before looking around to see where the girl was now. She was nowhere to be seen. Jack craned his neck, scanning the sky around him for any sign of movement. There was none.

The temptation was too great. He had to make one quick turn to see if he could catch another glimpse of her. Dipping the left wing slightly into a gentle climbing turn, he twisted as far as he could in order to scan the sky to the east. His immediate reward was a fantastic view of the first diamond rays of the sun, as it peeked its fiery head over the horizon. But there was something else as well: a strange swirling vortex like the one he had seen the first time he saw the dragons. It was behind him and lower, with a diameter barely larger than the dragons' wingspans, yet there they were – two, no, three of them. The dragons were heading straight for the vortex. Then they were gone. Just like that. The vortex collapsed in on itself the instant the final dragon entered, leaving no trace of their existence.

How did they do that and where did they go? he wondered.

One look at the expression on the spy's face in the front cockpit and Jack knew for certain that he was not delusional. The dragons were real. It was a relief. With someone else to back up his account, the senior officers might believe him this time. The man was not really dressed for high altitude flying, but Jack had no intention of risking the agent's life by flirting with ground fire. By flying higher they risked being engaged by enemy aircraft, but so long as they were quick about getting back across the lines . . .

'Oh, Lord!' he whispered suddenly, as realisation struck. 'How the devil am I going to write up this jaunt?'

## BRITISH WAR OFFICE MEMO

03-02-17

*Hugo*

*I need to see you re. Capt. Miller. His C.O. contacted me again. It appears he has reported another encounter with the 'dragons' he mentioned in that unusual combat report he filed last year. Ordinarily I'd dismiss it as nonsense. The strange thing is that a member of the Secret Service has corroborated his claims. I suggest that any correspondence on this matter be marked 'TOP SECRET' until we can determine what we are dealing with.*

*I've ordered Miller's C.O. to destroy the report he submitted. I think the less we commit to paper on this matter, the better.*

*I also suggest we meet ASAP to discuss. How are you fixed for tomorrow?*

*Maurice*

Lieutenant General Maurice Tremelayne

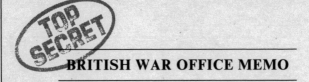

## BRITISH WAR OFFICE MEMO

03-02-17

Maurice

I absolutely agree on all counts. There is something most strange going on here. Tomorrow, 10.30am, your office. I'll see you there.

Hugo

Field Marshall Hugo Fitzpatrick

## Chapter Ten
# A Brief Respite

As they emerged into a deep valley in the midst of the mountain range, Elian was bathed in a sense of elation. He felt like a hero. They had saved the man in his flying machine from his enemies again, and they had done so as a team effort. *If we can work together like that for the rest of the quest, then our chances of success have got to improve,* he thought.

The only dampener to his feeling of triumph was the wave of fatigue he felt through his bond with Aurora. She was exhausted, and flying up here in the mountains would tax her further.

'*Looking at the sun, I'd say it's about late morning, Ra,*' he said. '*I sort of expected you to get us here as soon after we left Orupee as possible. Is it the same day, or have we lost more time?*'

'*We arrived here no more than a few heartbeats after*

leaving Orupee, Elian,' she replied. 'I was most careful about that. But you must remember that we have travelled a long way east in the instant we were away. The sun rises much earlier here.'

'Oh, I see,' Elian said, feeling foolish. 'Thanks, then ... um, let's see if we can find a suitable place to land,' he continued quickly. 'I can feel how tired you are. You need a rest after that effort. We've got plenty of time to find the night dragon enclave before nightfall.'

'A rest would be welcome,' Aurora replied. 'I shall tell the others and we will start looking for a good place.'

The mountains of Isaa were very different from those they had seen in Central Orupee and Northern Cemaria. There was a sense of remoteness about them unlike anything Elian had ever experienced. The range appeared vast and Elian could feel by the shortness of his breath that even though they were in a valley, they were flying much higher than he was used to. The white caps of the mountaintops extended a long way down from the peaks despite it being summer.

Gods, those peaks must be high! he thought, momentarily awestruck.

'They are the highest in all Areth,' Aurora informed him. 'Even dragons hesitate to fly over them.

*Very few of your kind can survive a flight so high. A number of riders have tried – through bravado, or plain foolishness. None have returned unscathed. It is best to enter and depart the range through one of the main passes, but the night dragons monitor these constantly. It is impossible to approach the enclave of the night dragons without passing the night dragon sentinels. Unless, of course, you ride a dawn dragon.'*

Aurora sounded smug as she continued. *'We are already within the range. My dragonsense brought us inside their domain. To my knowledge they have no further guard points short of the enclave. We should be able to get close without Segun's people detecting us. The only problem I foresee is getting out again. I've drawn too deeply on my powers to form any more gateways for a while, so we will have to risk alerting the sentinels.'*

*'Do you know how to get to the enclave from here?'* Elian asked, gasping as he struggled to speak aloud. The air burned cold inside his chest as his breathing automatically deepened and accelerated.

*'No, but Fang does. Do not fear. We shall find Pell and Shadow.'*

Kira was pleased when her dragon Fang slid forwards into the lead position. Elian and Aurora had led them through the gateways and drawn them into a struggle that was none of their business. Through the bond she could feel that Fang had suffered a large number of stings from the unnatural weapons in the other world. Her first priority was to find a place to land as soon as possible and to have Firestorm breathe his healing fire over her dragon.

No more distractions, she thought, rubbing at her side. The sympathetic pains she was feeling made her more determined than ever to keep the group focused. They needed to find Pell and get him to the griffins so that he could learn more about the night orb, and that was exactly what she intended to do. The hunter who was easily sidetracked rarely brought home the meat.

'Fang? Is there anywhere around here that we can stop without being seen by the night dragons?' she asked.

'Aurora just asked me the same question. There are few places here that offer much cover,' he replied. 'But I do know of one. It isn't far.'

'Good. I think we all need a short rest after this morning's adventure.'

Fang cruised along the valley at a fast glide, only beating his wings when it became a necessity. Unsurprisingly there were no signs of human habitation. The great peaks around them were majestic and awe-inspiring, but they offered little to mankind aside from a place to retreat from the rest of the world.

Is that why the night dragons have adopted it as their home? she wondered. The day dragon enclave had been quite accessible and hospitable. The thought made her wonder about the other enclaves, and the dusk dragon enclave in particular. It was in Ratalusia, and Ratalusia was a long way away. Will we need to visit the home of the dusk dragons, too? she mused to herself.

'*We've arrived,*' Fang said suddenly, his voice in her mind interrupting her thoughts.

Kira could see nothing welcoming in the bleak landscape, but as Fang descended, he turned purposefully to the left, towards an outcrop of rock. They touched down before Kira saw the entrance to a cave, concealed in the crook where the rocky ridge projected out from the base of the mountain.

'*Gods alive, Fang! How did you find this place?*' she asked aloud. '*I would never have spotted it.*'

'*That is because you are not a dragon,*' he responded, his tone aloof, but gently teasing. '*We have a certain affinity with caves . . . though, in truth, I found this one by chance when dodging night dragons during my last trip to this part of Areth.*'

The admission made Kira smile. She was quietly pleased that Fang had a sense of humour, given his formal speech and archaic code of honour. Dragons were strange creatures. Even though she had initially wanted to hate Fang for taking away her chance to be a hunter, she found herself caring deeply for him. Kira had vowed that she would never forgive him for destroying her dream, but the quest had given her the opportunity to be a part of a different kind of hunt.

The inner conflict tangled her mind and heart with a confusing mess of emotions. She envied Elian his enthusiastic thirst for adventure. Had she not been so close to her goal when Fang had come along, she might have enjoyed a similar attitude. Instead she felt forced to hide the little flame of resentment that continually burned inside.

Kira dismounted and let Fang lead the way. A refuge like this in such inhospitable terrain looked a likely lair for one of the larger mountain predators, but Fang was quick to report the cave empty. It was a bit of a squeeze for the dragons to enter through the mouth, but once they were past the threshold, the cave opened out into a chamber that was easily big enough to accommodate them all.

The riders went outside and found some large flat stones to use as seats. They had no torches, so they only dragged the stones as far as the mouth of the cave where it was light enough to see. The dragons were happy to lie in the darkness beyond, their eyes gleaming eerily from the deep shadows. The blue nimbus of Firestorm's healing breath lit the cave briefly as he healed Fang's bruised scales, giving the underground chamber a momentary feeling of enchantment.

Kira sighed as the nimbus faded and the cave returned to being a mundane hole in the cliff-wall. There was something magical about the day dragon's healing powers.

'*There is no magic in Firestorm's breath,*' Fang said quickly. '*His healing fire is a natural phenomenon. Fish can breathe under the water, but that doesn't make them magical. They were designed with the ability. Magic is unnatural and distorts the order set in place by the Creator's hand. It is dangerous, practised by foolish men who seek power and control over their surroundings. Mankind was not designed to handle such power. Neither were dragons. It is one of the major differences between our kinds that we dragons have more sense than to dabble with powers not meant for us.*'

'But if magic isn't meant for us, then who is it meant for?' Kira asked.

'*That is for the Creator to know, and for us to ponder,*' he replied.

'You're evading the question.'

'Yes.'

Kira burst out laughing, and the sound echoed around the cave. Elian and Nolita both turned to her with inquisitive expressions.

'What's so funny, Kira?' Elian asked.

'Dragons,' she replied. 'Dragons and their "holier than thou" attitudes. For all their years and experience, it's good to know they're as ignorant as we are about some things.'

Kira did not explain further, but continued to chuckle quietly to herself for a while. It felt good to laugh. She had not found anything much to laugh about for a long time. Her spirits felt lighter for it and with the nagging pain of Fang's wounds now gone, she began to feel much more positive about their situation.

'Would anyone like some hot food?' Nolita asked suddenly.

'We don't have any fuel for a fire,' Elian pointed out.

'I know,' she replied, her voice tentative as she explained. 'We won't need a fire. I could just eat a bit of fried mutton with some of Kira's herb mix right now. We'll need a plan if we're going to get into the enclave of the night dragons without causing trouble. And I always think better with a full stomach.'

'I won't argue with that,' Elian agreed, his

expression showing curiosity. 'And I'm intrigued to see how you intend to cook food without a fire.'

'So am I,' added Kira. She watched as Nolita gave them both a shy smile and flicked her blond hair back from her face.

'Actually it wasn't my idea,' Nolita said, sounding embarrassed. 'Here, give me a hand.'

She led them outside where she selected several large stones. Kira followed with Elian and a quick exchange of glances established that he was as bemused as she was. Between them, they carried the stones into the cave and then built them into a pile at Nolita's direction. With Elian's help Nolita laid a final large, flat stone across the top, testing it thoroughly to make sure it was stable.

'That should do it,' Nolita said, satisfied. 'Now I suggest we step outside for a moment, and bring our packs.'

'Whatever you say, Nolita,' Kira replied, her tone dubious. She looked across at Elian, who shrugged.

They all walked out into the open and paused. The breeze was chill, but the blue sky above showed no signs of rain.

'Over here.' Nolita beckoned them away from the mouth of the cave and down along the ridge-line.

'Where are we going, Nolita?' Kira asked. 'Is it far?'

'No, not far,' she replied. 'In fact, this should do nicely.'

Nolita stopped and looked back at the cave entrance. Kira glanced at Elian. He looked as confused as she felt. A sudden familiar roaring sound drew everyone's attention towards the cave entrance. Visible waves of heat rippled the air immediately outside the cave. The sound of Firestorm's roaring flames continued for a considerable time. When the resonating blast stopped, Nolita led the way back inside. The flat stone on the top of the stack was glowing red with heat.

'It's too hot to cook on at the moment,' she said, 'but Fire tells me it will be fine in a couple of minutes, and should continue to give off heat for some time. He says it's not the best rock for holding heat, but it will suffice for our needs. Who's going to do the cooking?'

'I will,' Kira replied. 'I've never cooked on a hot rock before.'

She watched, mildly amused, as Elian bowed and thanked Firestorm for his efforts. He was so polite it was funny sometimes.

'*He says it was his pleasure,*' Nolita informed Elian. Nolita ran her fingers through her hair. The

134

gesture was not like that of most girls. Rather than a subconscious preening, it almost looked as if she were digging gouges into her scalp with her fingernails. Kira had seen Nolita do it before – normally immediately after communicating with her dragon.

That must be it, Kira thought. It's another of her little cleansing rituals. What she thinks it will do, heaven only knows!

A few minutes later the aroma of sizzling meat filled the cave. Elian drew in a deep breath and sighed happily. Pangs of jealousy tweaked at Kira's heart. He looked so comfortable.

'Any ideas on how we approach the enclave, Elian?' she asked, deliberately dispelling the contented feeling of the moment.

His brows furrowed. 'Not really,' he admitted. 'We could just fly up to the entrance and ask to see Pell, I suppose.'

'We could, but I suspect that would end our hopes of completing the quest,' Kira replied, trying hard to keep the scorn she felt from her tone. The idea of offering up such an ill-thought-out suggestion appalled her.

Nolita nodded. 'Fire says he can't go anywhere near the enclave and hope to stay safe.' She sounded relieved.

'Fair enough,' Elian said, pursing his lips. 'Ra

tells me that the same goes for her and Fang, though surely Fang would have the best chance of getting close without being noticed. Especially if he approaches at dusk, when his camouflage is at its most effective.'

Kira looked into the darkness towards where she knew her dragon was lying. '*What do you think, Fang?*' she asked silently. '*Could you get into the enclave?*'

'*I could get you in, but I would not be able to stay,*' he replied. '*I could not conceal my presence for long. The night dragons would sense me, even with my camouflage at full effectiveness.*'

'He says he could get me in, but then he'd have to leave or the night dragons would find him,' she relayed to the others.

'Get *you* in?' Elian said immediately. 'Don't think for a heartbeat that you're leaving me behind, Kira. Fang managed to carry us both when he was injured. I'm sure he can carry us both now he's back to full strength.'

'You're not going to leave me here alone with . . .' Nolita didn't finish her sentence, but she did not need to. The fear in her voice filled in the missing words.

'It would be a lot safer here, Nolita,' Kira said soothingly.

'I don't care,' Nolita replied immediately. 'I want to come with you. Could Fang carry me too?'

'*I can carry you all,*' Fang confirmed to Kira. '*The enclave is not far from here. It is in a box canyon off this main valley a little way to the south. The problem will be getting you out again. I will not be able to remain close enough to hear you call if you get into trouble.*'

Kira related this information to the others and silence fell as they thought through possible solutions. To Kira's surprise, Nolita was first to offer up a possibility.

'Fire tells me that there's no chain or prison that could hold Shadow captive,' she said thoughtfully. 'So if they've imprisoned Pell, they'll be holding him somewhere that Shadow can't reach him. Shadow would never abandon Pell, so he'd effectively be tethered to the enclave until Pell found a way out.'

'That sounds logical,' Elian replied. 'But I don't see how it helps us.'

'Well, if Fang thinks he can get us in, then Shadow could fly us all out,' she said. 'She's much bigger than Fang. I imagine she could carry the three of us, and Pell, with ease. If we don't find Pell the quest will fail, but if we can get him to Shadow then we'll still have a chance.'

This is ridiculous, Kira decided. These two have no idea what they're talking us into.

'*If* we can find Pell. *If* we can free him. *If* we can get him to Shadow. That's a lot of ifs,' Kira said aloud, her tone sour.

'Have you got any better suggestions, Kira?' Elian asked. 'I'm not sure we've got much choice. Nolita's plan isn't watertight, but it could work.'

'It sounds about as full of holes as a colander,' she grumbled. 'But if I can't think of anything better by dusk, then I suppose we'll have to try it.'

## Chapter Eleven

# Into the Jaws

Kira watched silently as Elian ran through the sequence of sword strokes she had taught him. She had not wanted to get involved, but Elian had got the blade out and started waving it around as something to do whilst they were waiting for the sun to set.

It was a fine weapon. Kira had recognised that much from the moment she first saw it. The blade, once the property of the dragonhunter who had dogged their steps all the way from Racafi, was shaped from a length of dragonbone and was harder than any metal. Elian had picked it up from the meadow where, in their final confrontation, Shadow had eaten the dragonhunter. The man had taken Elian's sword from him during their first encounter, so there was a sense of justice in his keeping this one.

At first, Elian's efforts were painful to watch. To her eye he was now improving rapidly, though she was hardly qualified to judge. Few in her tribe carried swords, and none of those were masters with a blade. Hunters favoured spears and bows and had little time for close-quarter weapons.

She smiled slightly as memories of her own lessons surfaced. She had nagged Bemi, one of the more friendly hunters, to teach her swordplay. He had been kind enough to humour her, and they had spent many hours fencing with sticks, laughing at one another's mistakes and cheering the victories. It had been fun.

The smaller children often gathered to watch, so she and Bemi played to their audience. When defeated, the loser had to 'die' the most spectacular death they could, bringing squeals of delight from the young ones.

For Elian, however, drawing his blade would have more deadly consequences. How he would fare if faced with someone actually trying to kill him, she did not want to think about. His footwork looked all right when he was moving forwards and he was getting much faster with the practice patterns she had shown him. But when moving backwards he still looked clumsy and uncomfortable. The one major thing that would weigh in Elian's favour in a real fight was his sword. There was little that could stop a dragonbone blade. If he swung it hard enough, it would sheer straight through a metal one. Any swordsman would be thrown off guard by having his blade chopped in two.

The gloomy shadows around the mouth of the cave were beginning to deepen. It was time to go.

'Give it up, Elian,' she said, as he stumbled again during a retreating sequence. 'It's time we made a move.'

'It's no good,' he replied, slowing down and running through the sequence in slow motion one last time. 'I just can't seem to make my feet go where I want them to.'

'You won't learn to fence in a day,' Kira laughed. 'Much as I hate to admit it, you're doing a lot better than I did when my friend taught me. I don't recommend getting into any fights just yet, though. You'd be sliced and diced by any half-competent swordsman. You need proper lessons if you're going to be any good. I've only ever played with sticks.'

'How comforting!' he said sarcastically, carefully sheathing the sword and slipping the straps over his shoulders so that the scabbard seated comfortably against his back. 'I'll try to bear that in mind.'

The three young riders dressed themselves in the darkest colours they possessed. Their riding jackets were all made of similar dark grey leather, the perfect colour to blend in against the rocky crags. As a final effort at camouflage they each took strips of dark cloth cut from one of Kira's tunics and used them to cover the lower half of their faces and their foreheads, leaving just a slit for their eyes. Together they moved outside and Fang followed, leaving Firestorm and Aurora to rest.

'I'll take the saddle,' Kira said, her voice muffled by the cloth. 'Nolita, you sit behind me and Elian can sit behind you. I'd offer you the saddle, but I think you'll feel better being sandwiched between us when Fang uses his camouflage. It's quite un-nerving the first time your ride disappears from under you!'

Nolita nodded silently, but from what Kira could see of her eyes she could tell the girl was thankful. They all mounted, and Fang camouflaged before moving out into the open to begin his take-off run.

Kira would have preferred to leave Nolita behind. She suspected the girl would be a liability, but could not find it in her heart to force the issue.

One look at Nolita's face when she thought she was going to be left alone with the two dragons, and Kira knew they had to take her with them.

The blond rider held tight around Kira's waist from the moment she took her place on Fang's back, but squeezed even tighter when they started to move. Kira tensed her stomach against the pressure, but said nothing until they were safely airborne and climbing along the centre of the valley.

'You can ease off the death hug now, Nolita,' she called over her shoulder. 'There's very little wind. It shouldn't be too bumpy.'

Her prediction was correct. The air was smooth, though Kira soon grew to feel a little grateful for Nolita's closeness. She had not flown much by night and little enough at sundown. The mountains loomed larger than ever in the fast fading light of dusk, hulking over them, dark and menacing. There was a sense of brooding awareness hanging in the air that Kira knew to be her imagination playing tricks. Nevertheless, it felt as if at any moment one of the great peaks might reach out with an enormous rocky arm and crush them like bugs.

Don't be a fool, Kira, she told herself. You're far too old to be afraid of the dark.

They tracked along the great valley at speed. All sense of texture on the mountainsides gradually disappeared, leaving only deep black shadowy walls that seemed to climb away for ever. This was amplified when Fang suddenly plunged into the dark abyss of a narrow valley.

Kira instinctively held her breath as they entered the pitch-black void and she heard Nolita gasp behind her. The narrow band of sky above them was the only ribbon of reality. How Fang could see where he was going Kira had no idea, but he powered on and she sensed no hesitation in him through the bond. His confidence bolstered hers and for once she was truly glad of the intimacy of her alliance with Fang.

'*Nearly there,*' Fang warned.

For a moment Kira thought her mind was playing tricks on her, because there was something strange about his voice.

'*No, you're not imagining it,*' Fang said immediately. '*I've consciously narrowed our bond to reduce the chance of stray thoughts being picked up by the night dragons. The valley will open out when we round the next bend. I can already sense the presence of many dragons ahead, so I've shielded my thoughts to prevent our being discovered.*'

'*That makes sense,*' Kira replied, surprised to hear that her own mental voice had the same echoing quality as Fang's.

'I've also managed a quick private exchange with Shadow,' he continued. 'She is delighted that we've come to help. She and Pell arrived yesterday. Pell went in to see Segun, but she's had no contact with him since. She is worried that something has happened to him. She's going to cause a disturbance to draw the attention of the other dragons to let me get you in. Apparently Segun and five other senior riders left the enclave early this morning, but Widewing, Segun's dragon, would tell Shadow nothing about what was going on.'

'I think I can guess.'

'Yes, it seems we were right,' Fang observed. 'Shadow has given me an image of where Pell entered. She says the outer part of the cave appears empty now that Segun has left. Dropping you there is the best I can do. Find Pell and Shadow will try to bring you all back to where Firestorm and Aurora are resting. I will meet you there.'

'And if we can't find Pell?' Kira asked.

'Shadow won't leave without him.'

'Great! No pressure then.'

'We knew it wouldn't be easy, Kira,' Fang said, his voice calm. 'I have confidence in your abilities. You are a trained hunter. Use your skills. You will find him.'

It was so dark by now that Kira did not even realise they were turning left until the valley opened out ahead and the area of sky above lent more light to their path. As Fang levelled his wings, Kira experienced a strange feeling of disorientation. Her sense of balance told her that they were now turning right, but her eyes showed them to be flying straight. Her brain began to turn somersaults, trying to resolve the conflicting messages.

'*Relax, Kira,*' Fang told her softly. '*I've heard that you humans sometimes suffer this illusion. Riders call it "the leans". It is quite common. My wings are level. Close your eyes for a moment. Tell yourself we are flying level and then open your eyes again. The feeling will pass in a moment. That's what you get for having a body that's designed to work on the ground.*'

Fang's voice sounded mildly amused, but Kira found it anything but funny. If she could have chosen a time to discover a strange side-effect of flying, this would not have been it. A trumpeting roar sounded from somewhere in the darkness to her right.

'Don't worry,' she said quietly over her shoulder to Nolita, whose grip around her waist had tightened at the sound. 'That's Shadow creating a diversion for us.'

Shadow's roar demanded attention, and it seemed to be getting plenty. The air was suddenly full of night dragons, seeking to find out what all the fuss was about. The three riders crouched low on Fang's back as he weaved a silent path between them. When the air cleared of activity, Fang powered upwards.

The black cliff-wall that housed the enclave was dotted with the flickering glow of torches that shone from many of the open caves, but Fang climbed way above the inhabited openings. The darkness swelled ahead of them as they approached the face of the mountain. For a moment Kira thought they would crash headlong into the rock, but then she saw it. Ahead of them was an impossibly black maw, even darker than the deepest shadow of the cliff. She flinched and a shudder rippled down her spine as they passed between the great jaws of the rockface and it swallowed them with its dark silence.

They landed and Fang turned to face the exit before stopping to let them dismount. The three riders slid cautiously down his side, doing their best to make no sound as they landed. No sooner were they all down than Fang was on the move again, launching from the ledge and out into the night sky. They heard his great talons clicking across the stone floor of the cave and the slight whoosh as he launched, though there was no hint of a visual clue to mark his passage.

'All right, we're in,' Kira whispered. 'Let's see

what we're up against. We need to find a door out of here. There must be one somewhere towards the back of the cave. I'll take the left. Elian, take the right. Nolita, walk up the middle to the back wall and then turn whichever way you prefer.'

Step by careful step, they felt their way around the walls. It was Elian who came across the door. As soon as he felt the change of texture from stone to wood, he knew he had found it. Running his fingers back and forth it took but a moment more to find the handle. He felt around for a keyhole, but could not locate one.

'Hsst!' he hissed, quietly drawing the attention of the others. They joined him quickly and Kira patted him silently on the shoulder.

Elian stepped aside and allowed Kira to open the door. He was tempted to draw his sword, but he had enough sense to realise the desire was born from nervousness. He was more likely to injure one of his friends in the dark than to do anything useful with it, so he clenched his fists and concentrated on listening out for any sign of movement.

Kira turned the handle of the door and eased it open with infinite care. There was the slightest of creaks as she teased it open a crack, causing the three riders to wince in unison. A wedge of dim light spilled out through the gap, but there was no sound of movement on the other side. No one had noticed them yet. Heart thumping, Kira drew the door open further and peered inside.

A single burning torch lit the room beyond the door. It appeared to be a general living area, with comfortable chairs, a low table and several sets of shelves loaded with books around the walls. As far as Kira could see there were two other doors leading on from it, one in the wall ahead of her and another to her left. Aside from the lit torch there was no sign of life.

Kira stepped inside and the others followed. She instinctively turned towards the door to the left. If I was trying to keep a dragon and her rider apart, I would lock the rider as far out of reach as possible, she reasoned silently. This door would lead them deeper into the mountainside. As she reached for the handle, she paused and turned to face Elian and Nolita.

'Take off your face masks,' she ordered softly, beginning to unwind the material from her own face.

'But what if we meet someone?' Elian asked.

'We're going to bluff,' she whispered back. 'We'll need to speak to someone if we're going to get to Pell. We don't know where we're going, or how big this complex is. You saw how many caves there were in this cliff. There could be miles of passageways and hundreds of people. There's no way anyone here could hope to know everyone else. From now on we're night dragon riders sent by Segun to speak with Pell. Leave the talking to me. Don't say anything unless you have to. Just follow my lead.'

'All right, Kira,' Elian said with a slight shrug. 'It's your show.' He sounded unconvinced, but began removing the coverings from his face anyway. Nolita did the same.

They tucked the strips of cloth inside their jackets and once they were ready, Kira took a deep breath, gripped the handle and opened it with one swift movement.

## Chapter Twelve
# 'You're a Bad Girl, Kira!'

The sound of the key in the lock of the cell door brought Pell to his feet. The muscles in his legs bunched automatically in readiness as he felt the insane red heat of rage explode inside his gut. The door opened and the bright orange light of the guards' torches flooded the tiny cell.

Pell did not hesitate. Without pausing to see how many guards there were, or if they were armed, he put his head down and charged like an enraged bull. It was an act of unthinking madness that under different circumstances might have been effective. Unfortunately for Pell, the guards were particularly wary of new prisoners, so they were both alert and quick to respond.

The lead guard dodged Pell's charge with ease and stuck his foot out to trip him as he passed.

151

A second guard reacted faster still, clubbing him hard across his back with a cudgel as he tripped. Pell went down hard, rolling across the stone passageway and smashing into the opposite wall.

After nearly a full day in total darkness, his eyes could not cope with the sudden flare of light, so he never saw what hit him. Pain from the cudgel blow across his back was followed by more from his impact with the wall and a pummelling sequence of vicious kicks to his body from the guards. Pell curled into a ball, protecting his head as best he could with his forearms.

'*Shadow! Help me!*' he thought, pain lending power to his mental cry. No response. 'Gods, please!' he moaned aloud.

'Enough!' a deep voice ordered. 'Put him back inside.'

The kicking stopped and Pell gasped as hands dragged him roughly to his feet. He squinted, his eyes watering as he tried to focus. Blurry figures surrounded him, but he could not even count them before being flung back into the cramped cell. His lungs heaved erratically. He had taken a kick to the solar plexus that had temporarily robbed him of his breath.

'No more foolishness, Pell,' the deep voice continued. 'Our orders are to contain you, not hurt you. Now be a good lad. Eat your food and don't try anything stupid like that again. If you do, I won't be so quick to stop my men hurting you.'

Pell heard scrapes as a tray of food was placed on the floor inside the door of his cell. A moment later the door closed and he was plunged back into darkness, with only the faintest of glows visible under the base of the door.

He groaned as a cloud of despair engulfed him as completely as the darkness. His spontaneous break for freedom had been a disaster. The guards would be doubly careful from now on, making an escape less likely than ever.

Regaining control over his breathing was not easy, and the combination of pain, disappointment and frustration threatened to spark another involuntary response. His diaphragm fluttered as he fought to keep from vomiting. The smell of the food wafting across the cell made the feeling worse, and he swallowed several times in quick succession to clear the taste of sick from the back of his mouth. By sheer force of will, Pell maintained a fragile, but growing edge of control over his stomach. For several minutes, he stayed totally still, concentrating with fierce focus on making each breath slow and steady.

As his control over his body became more secure, anger built inside again like a raging fire. His mind raced as he imagined taking his revenge. I'll get my own back, he thought. Once I'm reunited with Shadow nothing on Areth will stop me.

Gradually the pain of his wounds dulled to a general throbbing. There were hot spots where some kicks had landed harder than others, but he used these as focus points for his anger as he began to move. Slowly, limb by limb, he uncurled his body and eased across the short distance to the tray of food. He did not feel like eating, but needed to drink. He had been dehydrated before his beating, but knew that more fluid would now flood the regions around his wounds. This would dehydrate him further.

Feeling ahead, Pell located first the tray, and then the beaker. Taking care not to spill the fluid it contained, he lifted it to his lips and sipped. His instinct was to gulp it down in one long draft, but again he exercised self-discipline and drank slowly, sipping the water and rolling it around in his mouth before swallowing.

Some time later, when he was sure he had finished the last drop, Pell carefully eased his body into a sitting position and leaned back against the side of his tiny cot bed. He felt dreadful. It was not just the physical pain, though that was bad. It was deeper than that – like a fist clamped around his heart and a cold lump of ice buried deep within his gut. His mind felt slow and helpless. It was almost as bad as the feelings he had experienced when he had fallen from Shadow's back. Then it dawned on him. He was afraid.

Kira strode through the door and into the passageway beyond as if she owned the night dragon enclave. Elian and Nolita followed in her wake, neither feeling nor looking anywhere near as confident as their companion. The passageway was empty, but they had taken no more than a dozen paces before a man emerged from a side door ahead of them. He saw them, but Kira did not react as he tensed, his eyes narrowing with suspicion under his dark brows.

'Who are you?' he demanded. 'And what are you doing here? This area belongs to Lord Segun and his council of senior riders.'

The man looked as if he had seen about thirty season rotations. He stood tall and straight, but he had a weak chin that took away any air of authority he might have otherwise commanded.

'I'm here on Lord Segun's orders, but who are you?' Kira retaliated, her voice every bit as challenging as the stranger's. 'You don't look like a rider to me, so what are you doing here?'

'I am Murvan,' he replied snootily. 'I'm not in riding gear because I live here. I'm both a senior rider and Lord Segun's personal assistant. You, however, I've never seen before.'

'Then you're just the person we're here to see,' Kira said, the challenge gone from her voice and replaced with a tone of purring sweetness. She held up her hand in the traditional gesture of greeting. 'My name is Ebony, rider of Sharpcry. My companions and I have not been riders long, so we were honoured when Lord Segun, together with five other senior riders, waved us down just beyond the Western Pass this afternoon. He sent us to fetch the prisoner, Pell.'

'Fetch him? Why?' Murvan asked suspiciously. 'Lord Segun was adamant this morning that Pell should be held prisoner.'

'Then he must have had a change of heart,' Kira replied with a casual shrug. 'He ordered us to take Pell and escort him to the mountain range in the north-westernmost area of Isaa. We are to fly as swiftly as possible and meet Lord Segun in the Valley of the Griffins.'

'Did he tell you why he was going there?'

'No,' Kira said. 'And it was not my place to ask.

Our orders are to get the prisoner there as fast as possible. Can you lead us to this Pell person?'

Kira kept her expression calm, though her stomach was turning somersaults inside. She knew she had placed Murvan in a difficult position, and his indecision was playing across his features.

From what little Kira knew of Segun, the man controlled the night dragon enclave with a fist of iron. She was counting on Murvan's fear of his leader. If he were close enough to Segun to be privy to what the night dragon leader was doing, then Murvan would have to assume she had spoken directly with his leader, or a member of his inner council. There was no other logical way she could know his movements so accurately. The precision of her story lent it credibility he would be brave to ignore. Segun's wrath was not something to be trifled with.

As Kira had hoped, Murvan did not take long to reach the conclusion she wanted.

'Follow me,' he said tersely. He whirled and swept off along the corridor, his long legs striding out so that the three companions were forced almost to run the first few paces to keep up.

Kira glanced back at the other two. Elian gave her a grin and a wink, but Nolita gave no indication that she had seen Kira's look. Her eyes were fixed on Murvan's back and she seemed only to have thoughts for where he was leading them.

As Kira suspected, the network of passages that Murvan led them through was extensive. They walked for several minutes in silence, turning first down one passageway and then another. Trying to keep a track of the turns became increasingly difficult, but Kira repeated the pattern over and over in her mind with a song-like rhythm as they went, adding each new turn to the mantra as they made it.

The presence of two guards in the final corridor gave the three young riders the clue that they had arrived.

'Halt! Who goes there?'

'It's Murvan, you fool! Surely you can see that?'

'Just doin' as I was told,' the guard replied, his voice full of reproach.

Murvan glanced upwards as if searching for divine help. 'You don't need to make the challenge if you recognise the . . . oh, never mind,' he replied, shaking his head in exasperation. 'Just open up. You're relieved. Lord Segun wants the prisoner released.'

'Yes, sir. No problem, sir. Right away, sir.'

Kira watched with concealed amusement at the exchange. Both guards were of heavy build, and apparently had limited intelligence. Their body language, the look in their eyes, their features, even the way the man with the keys fumbled to unhook them from his belt, indicated they were slow of thought. She was glad that they had Murvan with them to give the orders. Men like this would rather die than swerve one iota from their orders, and there would have been no chance of over-powering them.

As the guard rammed the key home into the lock and opened the door, Kira took a deep breath and strode into the cell. The success of this ploy was now totally dependent on Pell. If he gave the game away, things were likely to get difficult very quickly. The element of surprise might help them a little if it came to a fight, but she knew that their chances of winning a physical confrontation with the three men were not good. Worse, there were likely to be more guards within earshot.

'Is this the one?' The voice was hard, female and familiar. 'You're sure this is Pell?'

Pell crouched by the little cot bed, poised to fight like a cornered wolf. He was wary after his beating earlier, but he was alert to any chance of potential escape. It took a moment for him to make the connection and relate the voice to the person. It was

Kira! Kira? Here? And was that Elian and Nolita behind her? His mind whirled with confusion as he tried to imagine how they could have found him, and his eyes flicked back and forth between the guards and his fellow questors.

Kira seemed to be inspecting his face. No doubt he looked a mess after what the guards had done to him. He knew his left eye was swollen and he imagined there would be a fair amount of bruising. He wanted to say something, but the slight narrowing of her eyes gave him the clue that he should not show any sign of recognition. She and the others must have bluffed their way in here. Gods! he thought. They're braver than I gave them credit for.

'Yes, that's him,' Murvan confirmed.

'It's hard to imagine what Lord Segun wants *him* for,' Kira sneered. 'He looks pathetic to me.'

A fresh spark of anger flared inside Pell's gut. If he got out of here, she would pay for that comment.

'Don't underestimate him,' one of the guards said immediately. 'He tried to break out earlier. He's quite fast and strong.'

Despite his anger, Pell had enough self-control to stay silent. The Racafian girl had them wrapped around her little finger.

'Well if he knows what's good for him, he

160

won't do anything else that stupid,' Kira replied pointedly. She turned and Pell met her gaze. To his surprise he could not look into her eyes for more than a second or two before looking away. 'Lord Segun wants you to follow him to the Valley of the Griffins. Will you come willingly, or should we tie you?'

'I'll come,' Pell replied, his voice gruff even to his own ears. He lowered his eyes to the ground as if in defeat.

'Good,' Kira continued. 'I never did like unpleasantness. Where's his flying jacket? He'll need it. It's going to be colder than an ice dragon's heart where we're going.'

'It's over there.' One of the guards pointed to a bundle in the corner.

'Good. Come. We don't have all night. I don't want to keep Lord Segun waiting.'

Kira motioned to Elian and Nolita, who moved past her and helped Pell to his feet. He groaned as he straightened.

'Are you fit to ride?' she asked, giving him a raking look up and down.

She was mocking him again. He was sure of it. Damn you, Kira! You've had your fun. Don't push it! he thought, furious. 'I'll manage,' he growled, his anger and stubbornness warring for dominance.

161

'He's likely to give you trouble, Ebony,' Murvan observed. 'He's not exactly been a model prisoner. Would you like me to assign a few more riders to accompany you?'

'There's no need,' Kira said with a curt shake of her head. Pell winced as she flashed him a vicious glance. 'I think he's learned his lesson. Trust me. I promise you the three of us will keep him focused on following Lord Segun as fast as possible.'

Pell held his breath and did his best to look contrite as Murvan considered her response. It was hard to control his anger when Kira was being so deliberately provocative, but he realised he would have to save his response until a more opportune moment. Once they were out of the enclave, he would have plenty of time to teach her some respect.

Murvan did not look happy, but Kira continued to project confidence and authority. After a moment or two he caved in.

'Very well, Ebony. On your head be it. Just remember that I offered. If it all goes wrong, I don't want it said that I did not do everything in my power to help you.'

'Don't worry, Murvan,' Kira replied, giving him a warm smile. 'I'll make sure Lord Segun hears how helpful you've been.'

Oh, you're a bad girl, Kira! Pell thought, inwardly forced to admire her bravado.

'Would you mind leading us back?' she continued. 'I'm fairly certain I can remember all the turns, but it would be inconvenient to get lost – particularly as we're in such a hurry.'

'Of course,' Murvan replied. He turned to the two guards. 'You're relieved of duty, men. Report to the shift master at sunrise.'

'Yes, sir. Thank you, sir,' they replied together. The men took no chances on Murvan reconsidering his decision, but disappeared quickly out through the door and off along the passageway at speed. It was a well-honed response that brought a twitch of a smile to the corners of Pell's mouth. Even more amusing, though, was the irony of Murvan leading the rest of them out through the cell door and along the corridors towards the outside world.

## Chapter Thirteen
# The Sound of Silence

'*Shadow?*'

Nothing. Pell had called every few seconds since they left the cell. His memory of where the cell was in relation to the cave where Shadow had dropped him was vague, but he knew it would not take them long to reach it – a few minutes at most.

'*Shadow?*'

Murvan was leading them out through the maze of passageways with the confidence of one who was intimately acquainted with his surroundings. If they were going by the most direct route, then they must surely reach it soon, he thought.

'*Shadow?*'

'*Pell?*'

The reply was faint, but it was there. Shadow could hear him at last.

'*Shadow, I'm coming,*' he thought, concentrating as hard as he could on forming the words clearly in his mind and projecting them with all his might.

'*I'll be waiting,*' she replied. '*Are the others with you?*'

'*Yes, they're here. Did you bring them?*' he asked.

'*No, Pell. They came of their own accord. They knew you were in trouble. Fang got them into the enclave, but he had to leave to avoid being detected. I will be carrying you all out. We'll meet up with Fang, Fire and Aurora once we're well away from here.*'

So we're all reliant on Shadow to get us out, he realised. That put him straight into a position of strength. If the three riders had not taken such risks to come to his aid, he would have enjoyed this. It would be particularly sweet to pay Kira back for her recent comments. Unfortunately, he could not escape the fact that he was deep in their debt.

He glanced across at Nolita. She seemed remarkably calm. There was no sign of fear in her eyes. That surprised him. They were, after all, in the heart of the night dragon enclave. As the rider of a day dragon there were not many places in the world that offered her more danger. Where was the fearful wretch he had left in Orupee a week ago? There was something different about her. She had changed – grown. What had they been doing without him?

'*How did the others catch up with us, Shadow?*' he asked. '*Did they give up on their quest for the day orb and decide to follow us after all?*'

'*I don't know,*' Shadow responded. '*Speaking with Fang was risky. We did not want to alert other dragons to his presence, so we kept our exchanges to a minimum. I am as intrigued as you are. I thought they were set on going to the day dragon enclave. They must have changed their minds.*'

Shadow's voice was getting stronger and clearer. They must be getting nearer to the cave where he and Shadow had landed. Kira confirmed this thought moments later when she placed a hand on Murvan's shoulder and stopped him in his tracks.

'That's great, thanks, Murvan,' she said. 'I know where I am now. We've taken enough of your time.'

'No, I insist,' he replied firmly. 'It's only a little further. Come, I'll see you off. I just want to make sure Pell doesn't give you any trouble. Once you've left the enclave he's all yours, but I feel a certain responsibility to ensure you get safely underway.'

Unless Kira came up with a way to divert Murvan from coming with them to the outer cave, things could get ugly in a minute, Pell realised. The four of them could overwhelm the older rider easily enough, but if Shadow could now hear Pell clearly, then it was a fair bet that Murvan's dragon could hear his rider as well. With hindsight it might have been better to deal with the rider whilst they were still deep in the mountainside. That would have left them with the problem of finding their way out, but at least they would have had a chance to build a lead on any potential pursuers.

'Very well,' Kira said, dipping her head slightly in a semi-bow to acknowledge Murvan's authority. 'Lead on.'

The senior rider turned to lead the way, but before he had taken two steps Kira was in motion. Pell was impressed by the speed with which she whipped her heavy belt knife from its sheath, reversed it and smashed the metal handle hard into the base of Murvan's skull. The man folded to the floor as if every bone in his body had melted. Pell expected her to make a run for the exit, but instead Kira sprang to the fallen rider's side and felt his neck for a pulse.

'He'll live,' she announced, sounding relieved. 'Come on! Let's get out of here as fast as we can. There's no way of knowing if his dragon felt him fall. If she did, then getting out of here could get interesting. Pell, call Shadow. We need a lift.'

'Already done,' he said, pleased to be a step ahead of her. 'She's waiting and expecting to carry us all.'

Kira did not waste further words. She was up and off along the corridor at a sprint towards the door at the far end. It was not until he tried to follow Kira that Pell realised he could not run. He tried, but after a few paces had to drop back to a walk. It was too painful. His ribs felt as if they were on fire and his vision blurred. Elian and Nolita were quick to support him as he gasped and stumbled.

'Come on, Pell,' Elian urged, his voice nauseatingly upbeat and encouraging. 'It's not far from here.'

Pell did not respond. Instead, he concentrated on keeping his breathing shallow and even, and lengthened his stride into a purposeful walk.

They reached the door at the end. Kira had already opened it and was waiting for them in the cave beyond. So was Shadow. Pell's heart leaped with joy as he made out her outline against the very slightly lighter night sky beyond. As they passed through the doorway, he felt Nolita falter at his side.

Ah, he thought. So she hasn't improved *that* much.

'*Get up on my back, Pell,*' Shadow told him with

an edge of panic. '*The dragons outside suspect that something's wrong. We could be in for trouble.*'

He repeated the message to the others, but despite the urgency he conveyed, Nolita did not move. She froze, rooted to the spot as he moved forwards to Shadow's side. Much as it galled him to admit it, he needed the help Kira and Elian gave him, or he would have struggled to climb into the saddle.

Kira scrambled up Shadow's side and settled behind him while Elian went back for Nolita.

'Come on,' he urged her, grabbing her hand and pulling her towards the waiting dragon. 'We've got to get out of here.'

'She's so big!' Nolita breathed, her feet unresponsive and her hands shaking. 'So big!'

'Yes, she's big,' Elian repeated. 'And that's a good thing, Nolita. If she wasn't that big, we wouldn't get out of here. Now move, or I'll throw you over my shoulder and carry you.'

'Oh, gods!' she whispered. 'Can't you just leave me behind?'

'Nobody's leaving anyone behind,' Elian growled through gritted teeth. 'Now climb up, damn you! Now.'

Something in Elian's voice finally got through to Nolita. She reluctantly followed as Elian pulled her by her arm until they reached Shadow's foreleg. The slightest of hesitations signalled her last token resistance before climbing gingerly up Shadow's side and settling behind Pell and Kira.

Pell held his breath as Elian swung into position behind Nolita. There was no time to wait for him to get comfortable.

'*Let's go,*' he ordered Shadow silently.

In a heartbeat, she turned towards the mouth of the cave and the open night sky. Elian wobbled slightly before finding his balance. Pell looked over his shoulder to check that everyone was set. He saw Elian stretching around Nolita's waist, trying to get a firm hold of the ridge in front of her, but the ridge was too big to offer him a solid grip.

'You all right?' he asked.

'Tell Shadow to go,' Elian replied quickly. 'I'll be fine.'

A wailing screech from outside the cave mouth sent shivers down Pell's spine. It did not bode well. At least one night dragon was airborne. If the enclave was already roused against them, then they would not stand a chance.

'*What's happening, Shadow?*' he asked.

'*Rumours are spreading of something amiss,*' she replied. '*Hold on tight. This might get a little rough.*'

There was no time to pass on the warning to the

others. Shadow suddenly took several bounding steps and launched into the night sky. No sooner was she airborne than she began to beat her great wings with mighty strokes, powering upwards in an effort to gain the advantage of height over any dragon that might try to stop her. It proved a good tactic. A wave of spine-tingling screeches pierced the darkness below and the night air was suddenly full of the sound of whooshing dragons' wings.

'They will not pursue us far without their riders,' Shadow said confidently. 'But they know that to fetch the riders now will give us too much of a lead. If we can just get out of this canyon, we'll have a good chance.'

'Won't having four of us on your back put us at a disadvantage, Shadow?'

'It won't make it easy,' she admitted. 'But let's not look for problems. I am strong – far stronger than most.'

'How many are after us?' Pell asked, scanning the darkness for signs of movement.

'I would rather not count,' Shadow answered. 'You concentrate on staying on my back. I will worry about the other dragons.'

Shadow continued to climb at a tremendous rate. Pell sensed that even with four riders on her back, she was climbing faster than he had ever experienced before. He could feel her effort through the bond. His underarms ached in sympathy with her straining wing muscles.

The pressure change in his ears was another clue. He had got into the habit of swallowing regularly when climbing and descending to even out the pressure on his eardrums. The pain could be quite intense if the pressure built too much. Tonight he could hardly swallow fast enough. The pressure was building so quickly that no sooner did he swallow than he could feel it starting to increase again.

There was no question of talking to the others. Silence was their greatest asset. He knew instinctively that Shadow was about to employ her most impressive ability. Not all night dragons could do it, but Shadow had long since mastered the art of silent flying. As with Longfang's mastery of visual camouflage, Shadow's skill was so complete that she made the whispering flight of a hunting owl seem noisy by comparison.

With her purple-black scales, Shadow could disappear into the darkness every bit as effectively as Fang, for not so much as a breath of air would speak of her passage. When she employed her ability, it was as if she extended a bubble of silence about her. The only time she could not use it effectively was whilst climbing, which required high-powered wingbeats.

A slight movement caused Pell to look around sharply to his left. There was something there. He was sure of it. Was it another dragon? He could not tell.

'*Hang on.*'

It was not much of a warning, but it was more than the three riders behind him got. To Pell's surprise, rather than turn away from danger, Shadow banked sharply towards it. There was a sudden jar of impact as she struck, followed by a fast fading screech of rage. Pell saw nothing of the dragon they had attacked. It was too dark. All he could tell was that Shadow had succeeded in forcing their pursuer to lose a lot of height after the collision, as the source of the screech fell away from them at a considerable rate.

'*What did you do?*' he asked, craning his neck and scanning the sky for signs of further danger.

'*I flipped him,*' Shadow replied. '*I had to do it then or risk him gaining the advantage of height over me. It's hard to gain height when you are upside down.*'

'*Did he crash into the mountain?*'

'*No, but he lost too much height to pose us any further threat,*' Shadow said, sounding smug. '*The others will be more careful about how they approach us now, which is exactly as I had hoped. It's time to see just how good the other night dragons are.*'

Despite having experienced it many times before, the change in noise level was as astonishing to Pell as ever. His three companions gasped behind him and he grinned as he gave a whispered 'Shhhh' over his shoulder.

He remembered the first time that Shadow had demonstrated the ability to him. One moment the great whooshing of giant wingbeats filled his ears, the next ... nothing. Total silence. It was eerie. Tonight, however, rather than sending chills running down his spine, it brought a warming sense of comfort.

Shadow had long ago explained to him that whilst a night dragon's ability to see in the dark was good, it was not her first source of reference when flying. Rather like a bat, hearing became her primary sense in the dark. Unlike a bat, however, night dragons did not screech in order to generate echoes. Instead they had a separate sense of proximity that worked similarly, but on a totally different frequency from that of sound. In concert, these two closely allied senses built an image in the dragon's mind that when added to any visual cues created a three-dimensional picture of incredible completeness. Apparently Shadow's stealth ability was unusual because it was able to confuse a fellow night dragon's sense of proximity. Pell knew this made her ability special, but had never really seen its full effects until now.

No sooner had Shadow gone silent than she folded her wings and dropped suddenly. Pell's stomach lurched and his heart began to pound. They felt as though they were falling, although there was no sound of wind-rush. The solid reality of Shadow's back beneath the riders became an important source of reassurance as everything took on a strangely surreal feel.

Shadow did not drop far before she silently eased out her wings and arrowed in close to the right hand wall of the canyon, where the darkness was at its most intense. It was so dark here that although Pell knew Shadow was all but brushing her right wingtip against the rocky mountainside, he could see nothing of its dangerous proximity. He trusted Shadow completely. He could feel her confidence through the bond and he relaxed. She was in her element. It never crossed his mind to think how the others might be feeling.

The sounds of dragons in pursuit were obvious now that Shadow was flying so silently. There were some below and behind, at least two above and behind, and one that was flying almost alongside them in the middle of the canyon.

'*There's loads of them, Shadow!*' Pell said

tentatively through the bond. 'How are we going to shake them?'

'Don't worry, Pell,' she replied. 'There will be a degree of danger for the next few minutes, but I'm going to show them shortly that trying to follow me is not a good idea.'

## Chapter Fourteen
# Outlaws

As the tight canyon twisted and turned, so Shadow began to switch from one wall to the other. The first time she switched, she did it so subtly that Pell nearly failed to notice. The only clue was when she dipped underneath and behind a night dragon. She passed so close that Pell felt as if the dragon's tail might inadvertently swipe him out of the saddle.

In the instant that Shadow was directly below and behind the other dragon, she let slip a deliberate wingbeat noise designed to attract attention before continuing her silent slide across to the deep shadow of the opposite wall.

The results were spectacular. Before the unsuspecting dragon knew what was happening, several chasing dragons were stooping down on top of him with talons extended. The resulting melee was chaotic and noisy, allowing Shadow to abandon her silent flight and power upwards a few strokes, once again giving her the advantage of height over her pursuers.

Pell could feel her amusement through the bond as she changed back to silent flight again. She was actually enjoying this! The thought shocked him and a chill settled in the pit of his stomach. They were engaged in a deadly chase, being pursued by an unknown number of adversaries, and Shadow was having fun!

In the secret part of Pell's mind a question gnawed. Was his dragon completely sane? He had always known her desire for power and recognition matched his own, but tonight he was seeing a side of Shadow she had never shown him before.

The tangle of dragons in the centre of the canyon began to separate, but before the confusion had been totally sorted out, Shadow dived back in and stirred it up some more. In a deft move, she slid across the top of the fight and briefly locked her talons onto the wingtip of one of her would-be pursuers, unbalancing him such that he slewed sideways and collided with a second dragon. Both plummeted, briefly out of control, only to split a lower formation that was still climbing towards the fray.

The screeches of rage from the dragons needed no translation. Suddenly, the levity in Shadow's mind disappeared and Pell felt a terrible sadness through the bond.

'*What's wrong?*' he asked, worried.

'*One of the dragons below us just met her end,*' she replied, her voice cold and distant. '*I didn't mean to hurt her. It was an accident. I was trying to put them off following us.*'

'*Of course you were,*' Pell replied quickly. '*They weren't exactly playing friendly. With all those dragons in such a narrow canyon, confusion and collisions were always a danger.*'

'*Well, that's not quite true,*' Shadow admitted. '*But I appreciate your support. We need not worry about immediate pursuit any longer. They have called off the chase.*'

'*Great!*'

'*Don't get too excited,*' she warned. '*They'll be after us again soon enough. I was given a message from Sharptail, one of the older dragons. He called to me as the decision was made.*'

'*Really? What sort of message?*' Pell asked, intrigued.

'*A message of banishment,*' Shadow responded, her tone in his mind flat and emotionless. '*He made it clear that if either of us ever return to the night dragon enclave, we will be killed on sight. We have been declared outlaws.'*

Outlaws! It took a moment for the magnitude of the word to sink in. Outlaws! A week ago, when the Oracle had told them they would be undertaking the Great Quest, Pell's imagination had revelled in the glory such a prestigious life purpose would bring him. Had the Oracle foreseen this day? Had it known that the status Shadow and Pell craved would be cruelly denied at every turn? Pell had assumed from the outset that he had been chosen for his strength and potential. What if he had really been chosen because he was an outsider, different from all the others? There was a twisted sort of logic in that.

'Oh, gods!' he breathed. 'What have we done?'

'What's the matter, Pell?' Kira asked over his shoulder in a low voice. 'Is everything all right?'

What could he say? The situation was as far from all right as it could possibly be, yet his troubles were his own. The immediate danger was past.

'It's nothing, Kira,' he said eventually. 'They've turned back. We're in the clear for now. The dragons are returning to the enclave to get their riders. If they're going to chase us, then the real pursuit won't begin again for a little while.'

'Excellent!' Kira said, her voice a little louder this time.

Shadow was still employing her unusual talent for stealth. As a result the word sounded strange, almost dead, in the cocoon of silence that surrounded them. Kira intended to ask more, but a shiver ran down her spine when her voice was killed by Shadow's eerie ability.

By the time they emerged from the narrow canyon into the wide valley beyond, Pell felt thoroughly miserable. What good would it do to complete the quest now? Even if he did overtake Segun and get the night orb, there would be no glory in it. He had no standing at the night dragon enclave. He would have to avoid all contact with other night dragons and their riders for ever. Outcast! Pariah! Outlaw! The words bounced around in his head as the implications of the last few minutes started to sink in.

Stars pricked the sky overhead and the early moon was just visible over the southern mountaintops in the wider expanse of sky. They turned left and began to track along the near side of the great valley basin.

A chill wind breathed down the mountainside and Pell instinctively hunched in the saddle, trying to shoulder the cold aside. The wind would get stronger as the night wore on. He would need extra layers soon, or risk freezing. It was something he had seen in the mountains many times before.

By day the sun warmed the air in the valleys, causing it to rise. The result was a light flow of thermals up the mountainsides in the late morning and afternoon, but this breeze was invariably weak and capricious. By night, however, the opposite was true. Cold air at the top of the mountains sank, rolling down the slopes with gathering momentum to flow out along the valleys. The resulting wind was cold, and the effect was more pronounced than the daytime heating, giving rise to far stronger breezes. In certain valleys, the resulting wind could become very strong, particularly if the valley narrowed like a funnel. This accelerated the air still further, sometimes even to speeds normally only experienced around severe storms.

The dangers associated with the chill night breeze were not lost on Pell, but he did not care. The frosty gusts fitted Pell's mood. Even as his body tensed against them, his mind embraced their icy intent. For a moment he wished the wind could freeze the anguish from his heart, but he knew there was no such easy fix for this problem.

The more he thought about it, the more he felt

this whole situation was the Oracle's fault. Perhaps Segun was right. If he and Shadow had not been given this ridiculous quest, none of this would have happened. With their combined strength, they would have prospered at whatever they had put their minds to. Perhaps they still could. If they abandoned the quest and started again somewhere a long way from the night dragon enclave, they might still enjoy a fulfilling life together.

Pell could feel Shadow in his mind. He was sure she knew what he was thinking and she was saying nothing. Did this mean she agreed with him? He wanted to believe she saw things his way, but his gut feeling told him she was not happy. He knew how strong the pull to the Oracle was for her. Would she be willing to give up on the quest if he asked her to?

They began descending. He could see very little in the darkness, but he guessed they were approaching the place where the other dragons were waiting. Swift and silent they swooped down to land by an outcrop of rock. The cave entrance was well hidden. He did not see it until the other dragons began to emerge, no doubt at the silent calls from their riders.

Elian and Kira slid down Shadow's side and ran straight to greet Aurora and Fang with affection.

Nolita also dismounted swiftly, but instead of running to Firestorm she moved away from the dragons and started emptying her water bottle over her hands. Pell dismounted more slowly, nursing his bruised body to the ground. His fingers lingered on Shadow's scales as he fought with his emotions.

Suddenly Kira stiffened. Reading anger in her body language took no great skill. Whirling from where she had been stroking Fang's face, she covered the short distance back to where Pell was standing in what seemed like a handful of furious steps. Hands on hips she confronted him, eyes blazing.

'What the hell do you think you're doing, Pell?' she snarled.

'I'm not sure I follow you, Kira,' he replied, confused. Gritting his teeth against the pain it brought, he straightened to his full height.

'Fang tells me you're considering abandoning the quest,' she spat. 'Shadow felt you would do better to air your thinking publicly. It seems your dragon has a lot more sense than you do.'

Feelings of betrayal and shock rocked him. He looked up at Shadow in disbelief. How could she do this to him?

'*We cannot blame the Oracle for this, Pell.*' Shadow's voice in his head was stern and sure.

The flash of anger he directed at his dragon was fierce. He would never have believed her capable of sharing his thoughts with another like this.

'Why not?' he asked her aloud, his voice laced with fury. 'We wouldn't be in this situation if it wasn't for the Oracle's damned quest.'

'*It was our choice to undertake the quest,*' she pointed out. '*Like it or not, we have to take responsibility for that decision. This is not the Oracle's fault. It is a situation of our own making. We have both acted without considering the consequences of our deeds.*'

'The Oracle's "damned" quest is the reason your dragon exists,' Kira said fiercely. 'It's the reason all of our dragons exist. That's what this is all about.'

'The quest is a nonsense,' he responded bitterly, turning on Kira as the easier target for his anger. The red fury he felt temporarily masked his physical pain.

'Then why did you agree to it with such enthusiasm?' Kira asked. 'No! Let me tell you. The truth is you agreed because it fitted your expectations: glory and honour. Don't deny it. It was written all over your face.'

'Yes, I saw it as my big chance,' Pell growled. 'Shadow and I both did. And now any chance of good coming from this is gone, so why bother? It's all a nonsense.'

'Good for who?' Kira stormed. 'Good for you! You selfish son of a—'

'Go ahead. Swear all you like,' Pell mocked. 'Come on, Kira. Tell me your motives for following this quest are pure. At least I'm honest about my intentions. Why don't you tell us *your* reasons for agreeing to the Oracle's mad errand? And don't give me any pap about saving dragonkind. Save that for Elian.'

Elian looked confused, but Kira's eyes narrowed and her hand went instinctively to her belt knife. Pell did not flinch. He just smiled.

'My actions are not in question here,' she replied, her voice icy. 'Yours are. All that talk back at the campsite near the Oracle's cave was just noise, wasn't it, Pell? *I'm not afraid of* anything, she mimicked. 'I can't believe you had the gall to let those words out of your mouth! The moment things turn tough you want to run away. I'm surprised you aren't crying out for your mother. Gods, I wish you'd been there when Nolita retrieved the day orb! Maybe then you'd have some understanding of what bravery is really all about.'

'When Nolita *what*?' Pell exclaimed.

'You heard me.'

'Impossible!' he spat. 'Just to get to the day dragon enclave would have taken you . . .'

186

'... five days,' Kira finished. 'Yes, but with Aurora's ability to transport us between worlds we made up a lot of time on the way back and in catching up with you.'

Pell looked around at Nolita in disbelief. She was scrubbing at her hands, occasionally glancing up at the two arguing riders. As soon as she realised Pell was looking at her, she looked down and concentrated on her hands again. He shook his head. It did not seem possible. Yet why would Kira lie? One question from Shadow to the other dragons confirmed what she said. The dragons did not lie to one another.

'*So what would you have us do?*' Shadow asked. '*Run? Hide?*'

'*I don't know,*' he said. '*I need to think on it.*'

'*Well think well, and think quickly, rider,*' she replied, her voice fierce with anger. '*The quest is alive. We are free. Your only crime amounts to having disagreed with Segun. I have killed another dragon. Living with that will not be easy. I will find it easier to justify if we complete the quest. It will give her death purpose. I'm sorry to upset you by involving the others in this, but it's important, Pell. The quest is not ours alone. If we walk away, the quest fails. We need to think beyond ourselves this time.*'

'Nolita was brilliant,' Elian was saying

enthusiastically, his words tumbling over the top of Shadow's. 'You should have seen it. She faced her worst fears, Pell. The Oracle's rhyme came true. It was a trial. Maybe what has happened so far is a part of yours. I don't know. One thing's for sure, I don't want to see Nolita's efforts amount to nothing. We've come a long way and risked a lot to find you and help you face your challenge. You can't give up now.'

'*Without the promise of glory the quest does not have the same lustre,*' Shadow admitted in his mind. '*But does that mean it is any less worthy a goal for us? We have been outlawed. If we cannot attain glory and renown within the enclave, then perhaps we should look to gain fame and notoriety by denying Segun what he wants.*'

The suggestion was so outrageous that for a moment Pell was left mentally speechless. His mind whirled. There was a certain allure to the idea: Pell, the rogue outlaw, fighting to right the wrongs of the corrupt institution. He had not flinched from the possibility of danger on the Oracle's quest, so why did he hesitate now?

Shadow was right. It had been his choice to defy Segun that had seen him imprisoned. Shadow's actions in the canyon had not really made the situation much worse. If he had bowed to the night dragon leader's will in the first place, he and Shadow would have taken their first step on the ladder to power. Had the reason for his defiance changed? No. He had felt then that Segun was wrong. The Oracle's intentions felt wholesome. They transcended the motives of men and dragons. Just thinking about the Oracle filled him with a special feeling.

'All right,' he said slowly. 'We press on with the quest, but only on one condition.'

'Really?' Kira responded, her voice dripping sarcasm. 'What makes you think you can set conditions, Pell?'

'Cool it, Kira,' Elian said soothingly. 'Hear him out.'

'My condition is simple,' Pell said, his eyes locked with Kira's. 'I lead. At least until we get the night orb.'

To his surprise, Kira burst out laughing. Pell glanced at Elian. The dawn dragonrider's reaction matched his.

'Do you have a problem with that, Kira?' he asked coldly.

'No,' she laughed. 'Not at all. Which way would you like us to go first, O Worthy Leader of the Great Quest? Do you have any clue where we're heading, or would you like your faithful followers to tell you so you can lead the way?'

'Enough, Kira!' Elian's command surprised everyone. Even Nolita looked up with respect at the power in his voice. 'Pell, have you learned nothing? We're in this together. We don't need a leader. We need to cooperate and combine our strengths. Each of us must be ready to step forwards and take the lead as the quest requires, but we were all chosen for a reason. Nolita and Firestorm have demonstrated their bravery. Kira and Fang have shown ingenuity, guile and gall in the way they led your rescue. Ra and I have led the others through another world to make up time. All you've done so far is to jeopardise the quest. Kira is right. You're in no position to make demands, but neither should she provoke you into further argument.'

Pell seethed inside, but despite his anger he could feel Elian was right. Kira's lips were pursed tightly together as she also fought to control a further outburst.

'Fang knows the way to the "brave ones" mentioned in the Oracle's rhyme,' Elian continued after a short pause. 'I suggest he leads us there. Before we go, though, we need to consider how we're going to get out of here without attracting more attention from the night dragons.'

'Shadow can get past the watchers without being seen,' Pell said quickly.

'As can Fang,' Kira pointed out.

'But Fire and Ra will be seen for sure,' Elian said thoughtfully.

*'We can fly out over the mountaintops,'* Aurora interjected. *'If you double up with Pell on Shadow, Nolita can fly with Kira. Fire and I will go the high route and meet you once you're well clear of the watchers.'*

Elian nodded. *'That makes a lot of sense. Thank you, Ra.'* He relayed Aurora's suggestion to the others, who all agreed it was a good idea.

As the heat of anger finally died in Pell's gut, so the pain of his physical wounds washed over him again. Even as he turned to remount Shadow the world spun out of control. There was no time to call out – no time for anything. The darkness took him and he fell.

## Chapter Fifteen
# Doubling Up

As Pell surfaced, he stretched. It was a self-satisfied stretch, like a cat waking from a snooze in front of an open fire and luxuriating in the lazy heat. He felt good. Incredibly good! He drew in a deep breath and tasted the clean mountain air as it passed over his tongue. It was fresh and invigorating. Then he remembered.

His eyes snapped open. He was outside. The ground under his body was far from comfortable. Elian, Kira and Nolita were all looking down at him. Elian and Nolita looked pleased, while Kira's expression was unreadable. What had happened? He couldn't make sense of it. They were outside the cave where they had met with the other dragons. It was still dark. How long had he been unconscious? He felt rested, as if he had slept for days. The pain had gone. He ran his fingers tentatively across the areas where the bruising had been worst. Nothing. He prodded harder: still no pain.

'I don't understand. What happened?' he asked, climbing to his feet and testing each limb in turn as he continued to check his body.

'Firestorm healed you,' Nolita said. Her voice sounded strange. It was as if she was torn between being delighted and scared.

Pell could sense Shadow's displeasure through the bond. *'What is she on about?'* he asked her silently.

*'When they are so moved, day dragons can imbue their fire with healing qualities,'* she said, her tone cold. *'Firestorm breathed such a healing flame over your body.'*

*'So why aren't you happy?'* he asked. *'I feel great. Isn't that a good thing?'*

*'I'm mindful that day dragons have little history of healing when it comes to night dragons and their riders,'* she stated coldly. *'They say the healing powers are incompatible with a night dragon's physiology, but I know of none who have confirmed this claim. The long history of enmity between our enclaves is not without reason. You saw the sort of flames Fire hurled at the dragonhunters. Seeing Firestorm heal you reminded me that my brothers and sisters are more familiar with the destructive day dragon flame.'*

193

'Well let's be thankful that Firestorm is friendly then,' Pell said. 'I can't remember the last time I felt this good.'

The initial sense of confusion had passed. He knew now what he had to do.

'Please thank Firestorm for me,' he said aloud, bowing first to Nolita and then to her dragon. 'I can't tell you how glad I am to be free of the pain.'

Nolita blushed and lowered her eyes, glad that the darkness was masking her embarrassment. 'Fire says it was his pleasure to help,' she mumbled a few seconds later.

'Enough!' Kira snapped. 'We need to get out of here. I suggest we mount up and get going before we have the entire night dragon enclave breathing down our necks.'

'Sounds good to me,' Pell replied. He noticed Kira's eyes narrow as she tried to determine if he was mocking her again. Giving her no time to react, Pell leaped up Shadow's side. No sooner was he in his saddle than he reached down to give Elian a hand up into position behind him.

After her admonition to get moving, Kira did not want to appear foolish by delaying. Within a few heartbeats she was also in position. Nolita hesitated, but followed her reluctantly up onto

Fang's back. The four dragons launched in quick succession. Shadow led briefly, but Fang eased ahead of her before suddenly disappearing as he employed his camouflage. Unburdened by riders, Fire and Aurora climbed quickly past them. Their wings were beating hard as they sought to gain height as rapidly as possible. Pell followed their progress for a while until their outlines were lost in the black mantle of the night sky.

Shadow and Fang had to fly back past the entrance to the canyon that housed the night dragon enclave. They angled across to the opposite side of the main valley, staying as far from potential trouble as possible. Pell stared into the black throat of the narrow valley as they passed, half expecting to see a huge flight of dragons pour out towards them at any second.

He told himself that the nervous fluttering in the pit of his stomach was excitement, but in his heart he knew the truth. The thought of going back to his cell, or worse, caused his buttocks to clench and his fingers to tighten their grip on the pommel. He was afraid. Denial worked to a degree, but he could not ignore the fear for ever. Would he end up like Nolita?

'*You will never be like Nolita,*' Shadow said suddenly.

Pell was startled. He had not intended his dragon to hear his thoughts.

'*Fear can be a healthy response to a dangerous situation,*' she continued. '*As long as one keeps it under control. You are too strong to allow fear to overwhelm you. Nolita's fears are largely irrational. There is a big difference.*'

'So long as you don't feel I'm turning into a coward,' he replied. '*I don't think I could bear it if you started to think of me that way.*'

'Not at all, Pell,' she said. '*I know your heart. You are brave and strong – a worthy dragonrider. Our path together has taken an unforeseen twist, but I feel no diminishment in our future. We continue on the road to greatness. Believe in this. Trust me. It will help.*'

*On the road to greatness* – he liked the sound of that. They were some distance past the enclave valley entrance now and there was no obvious sign of pursuit. But Shadow was taking no chances. She was employing her skills in stealthy flying to the full, cloaked in her strange bubble of silence and hugging the deep darkness near the steep slope of the main valley wall. Pell had lost track of Kira and Nolita, but he could just make out the sound of Fang's wingbeats so he knew they were not far away.

'Do you think riders from the enclave are following, Pell?'

Elian's voice sounded flat and dead in the silence surrounding them.

'They will come,' Pell replied softly. 'Even if they're not after us yet, they will be. I wouldn't like to guess how many will follow, but the night enclave will not let us get away easily. Once they work out what has happened, they'll be buzzing like a nest of angry hornets.'

'Not a pretty picture,' Elian noted.

'Quite! The faster we get out of the mountains and away from here, the better. The further we can get, the wider they will have to spread their resources to find us. There are a lot of night dragons, but they won't be able to cover all possibilities.'

'Ah, yes,' Elian replied hesitantly. 'About that . . . they might not have to spread themselves as thin as you imagine.'

'What do you mean?' Pell asked, twisting in the saddle in an effort to see Elian's face.

'Um . . . well . . . Kira told Murvan where we were heading, so they won't need to spread out so much.'

'She did *what?*'

'Don't get the wrong idea, Pell,' Elian said quickly. 'She had to tell him in order to establish our credibility. It was only because she showed that she knew where Segun was going that Murvan believed our story. Kira was brilliant. She played Murvan like a maestro. Unfortunately it won't take a genius to work out that we'll be following Segun northwest.'

'Damn!' he muttered. 'That changes things.'

'*Is there a problem, Pell?*' Shadow asked.

Pell told her what Elian had said.

'*I'll go through our options with Fang,*' Shadow told him, her voice sounding unflustered by the news. '*Don't worry. We'll work something out. Ask Elian where we're going. The other dragons haven't told me anything yet.*'

Pell had been so caught up in the escape that he had not thought to ask anything about where they were going, or who the 'brave ones' were. Northwest – what was northwest of here? The majority of the northern part of the continent was bleak tundra. There was another mountain range in the far northwestern corner of Isaa that was locked in a perpetual winter. It would be an extremely hostile environment in which to exist and he had never heard of dragons living there. He doubted anyone would live there by choice. He was reluctant to demonstrate his ignorance to Elian, but he was left with no option.

'Griffins!' he exclaimed softly when Elian told him what they had learned. 'I'd never have thought of griffins. It makes sense, though: half lion, half eagle – brave and proud. And they live in the mountains up in northwest Isaa? I didn't know that. I wonder how they came to be guardians of the night orb.'

'That was something we didn't discover,' Elian admitted. 'We don't even know for certain that they have it. But with Segun a day ahead of us and an unknown number of night dragons following us, we're likely to become the filling of a most uncomfortable sandwich before we get a chance to find out.'

The temperature was still dropping and the chill night breeze was picking up strength. A shiver ran down Pell's back, but his body's reaction was not due to the weather.

With the increasing wind helping them down the valleys, they were covering ground at an impressive rate. Pell could feel Shadow's concentration as she maintained total silence the entire way. They were approaching the pass that would take them clear of the mountain range. Even in the dark he recognised the shape of the descending valley ahead. The dragons and riders who guarded the pass were high up on the shoulders of either side of the mountains. Different riders used different vantage points to carry out their duties. There was no telling where they might be.

As they entered the pass, Shadow descended and tucked in tighter than ever to the left wall of the valley. Keeping to the darkest shadows, she skimmed the rock surface with breathtaking accuracy. Pell could no longer hear Fang and had seen no sign of Kira and Nolita for some time.

'Where are the others?' he asked Shadow tentatively.

'They've gone the high route,' she replied, her voice echoing strangely in his mind. 'They're trying to exit the pass at a level above the watchers. That way Nolita and Kira will be completely concealed by Fang's camouflage. Hold your silence until we're clear, or until they spot us. I don't want to draw attention unnecessarily. We're going to try to bluff our way out. I'm hoping that a night dragon leaving the range will not arouse the guard dragons' interest.'

As they descended along the widening pass, the great moon lit the valley ahead with its pale, silvery light. The cross light from one of the two minor moons added a further complication as the shadows on the left side of the valley thinned out. There was nowhere ahead dark enough for Shadow to disappear into. No matter which side of the valley she flew, her black outline was going to stand out against the moonlit countryside.

Realising the futility of attempting to remain

unseen, they slid out into the very middle of the valley, in plain sight of the watchers, but using the steep descending slope of the valley basin to pick up speed. Pell's eyes narrowed as Shadow began to accelerate. Their airspeed was building fast, making it difficult for him to see without squinting. His dragon's ability to deaden sound made the experience particularly surreal as the wind around him increased without the usual rushing noise of high-speed flight.

Shadow seemed to be gambling on the watchers' attention being focused outwards from the mountains and not noticing her until it was too late for an effective interception. It was a risky tactic. If they spotted her early, then the two watch dragons would hold all the advantages.

Pell flattened himself as best he could against Shadow's back and he could feel Elian doing the same behind him.

'The watchers have seen us already,' Shadow said suddenly, her voice grim. 'They're getting airborne. Hold on tight. This might get interesting.'

Shadow continued to accelerate, no longer just using the descending track of the valley, but also trading her height above the ground for more and more speed. In what felt like no time at all, the rocky ground seemed to swell up around them like a rising flood. Rocks and bushes began to whip past barely below eye level as Shadow flew lower than either of the riders had ever experienced before. The feeling of speed was unlike anything Pell or Elian had ever imagined, and was heightened by the limited visibility offered by the moonlight. The ride was initially smooth, but as their speed peaked and their height above the ground reached a natural limit, so it also became bumpy. Shadow had to react with fast, minute adjustments of her wings to hug the contours of the valley.

The next few minutes of flight were the most exhilarating Pell had ever known. The bumps and sudden dips, combined with the silent wind and the eerie scenery racing past at phenomenal speed, made him feel as if he were in a dream. Although he knew that if Shadow made the slightest mistake they would be unlikely to survive the impact, his trust in Shadow was so complete that he felt strangely comfortable with the danger. He was at one with Shadow and her fierce concentration. It did not cross his mind to think how Elian felt.

'Here they come.'

Pell craned his head around to see the incoming dragons, but he could make out nothing. An unearthly screech split the air behind and above them. It was loud, but it sounded more frustrated than threatening. A second dragon added its voice. This one sounded even further back than the first.

'As I expected,' Shadow observed, her voice sounding smug. 'Their caution has lost them the advantage of energy. They descended too rapidly, trying to drop in directly on top of us. To begin with they did not realise just how close to the ground we were. As they got lower, the dragons' sense of self-preservation got the better of them. They should have used their height to get ahead of us, but they erred. Now they've killed all their potential energy, and they don't have enough speed to catch us.'

'Did they speak with you?' Pell asked.

'They asked me to stop and answer some questions,' she replied. 'I ignored their request. It seems Segun has left new orders with the guards. Dragons entering or leaving the range must now explain the nature of their journey. I could have made something up, but we dragons are terrible liars. Also, I didn't want to risk other dragons catching us up whilst we tried to bluff the guards. Things could have turned very ugly if we had stopped to explain ourselves.'

Shadow eased slightly higher above the ground and began to accelerate forwards still faster, her powerful wings driving them on down the valley with great sweeping strokes. Pell glanced back over his shoulder again, but he could still not see their pursuers.

'We're clear,' he told Elian aloud. 'The guard dragons will never catch us now.'

'Good,' Elian responded, his voice tight with relief. 'I think I've had my fill of excitement for one day.'

## Chapter Sixteen
# Dangerous Entertainment

Kira felt almost comfortable as Fang descended into formation alongside Shadow. For the first time in a while she was back in familiar territory. They were involved in a hunt – well, more of a chase, or a race, depending on one's viewpoint, but the principles were similar. There was the added complication that whilst they were chasing down Segun in a race to the Valley of the Griffins, the four companions were in turn being hunted by an unknown number of night dragons.

Translating their circumstances into the frame-work of a hunt put her at ease with this new phase of their quest. There would be danger, but that went hand in hand with a hunt. Rather than dwelling on the negatives, Kira began to think through the practical things they could do to improve their chances of success.

A hunter had to master many disciplines: endurance, patience, stealth, strength, focus and, in the final moments, accuracy with weapons. Kira had trained her mind and body in these disciplines for season after season, but her companions would need guidance if they were to complete their mission and return to the Oracle with the second orb. Elian and Nolita were malleable enough, but Pell was going to be a problem. He was so absorbed with leading that he was likely to oppose anything Kira said, no matter how sensible. Pell had set her teeth on edge from the moment he first spoke to her, but she knew that continually clashing with him would not help their cause.

Gods but he's annoying! she thought. But I mustn't let him get to me. The trick will be to make him think we're all following his lead and listening to his ideas, whilst guiding him along a sensible path. If he wasn't so pigheaded, it would be easy.

'*Thinking about Pell, Kira?*'

'*How did you guess?*'

'*I've not yet seen anything else fire your mind with such angry frustration,*' Fang observed with wry amusement. '*You and he are alike in many ways. It is inevitable that you will clash.*'

'*I am nothing like Pell!*' she said, outraged by the suggestion. '*How can you even think such a thing?*'

'*I meant no offence, Kira,*' Fang replied, unrepentant. '*But the two of you are strong-willed, determined, and focused on your goals. Where you differ is in the nature of your ambition. Shadow is quite similar as well, but I venture she is more willing to listen to reason than either of you riders. If I heard correctly, you are thinking about manipulating Pell into following your lead by fooling him into believing he is dictating our path.*'

'*That's right.*'

'*Your best avenue to achieve that end is through Shadow,*' Fang suggested. '*Pell listens to her, and Shadow respects my age and experience. I can plant ideas in her mind that she will relate to Pell. He will then do as you wish, but think he and Shadow are doing all the work. Be warned: it will be frustrating to see him take all the credit. You will need to exercise considerable self-control to make it work.*'

'*I'll cope,*' Kira said quickly.

'*I hope so,*' Fang replied. '*Because if you lose your temper and give the game away, he will develop a whole new level of wariness.*'

Kira fell to thinking about that for some time. It was true, she realised. Despite all the discipline she had learned with the hunters of her tribe, she was still quick to feel anger. Holding herself in check might not be as easy as she thought, but she would only need to do it until they got the night orb. Once they had that, the search would move on to the dusk orb and all Pell's arguments for being leader would no longer have any weight.

The two trios flew on into the night, holding a steady course to the north and west of the great mountain range that housed the night dragon enclave. Kira's thoughts wandered as she became lost, staring with renewed wonder at the beauty of the starlit sky. The third moon, Tritos, was climbing now, its pale blue face round and chill – very different from the silvery hue of the great moon and the pinkish shade of Bimodar, the other minor moon. A shooting star flashed across the heavens, followed swiftly by a second. Her breath caught in her throat. No matter how much she stared at the stars they never failed to fill her with a sense of awe.

'*I think you should know that Firestorm and Aurora are above us.*' Fang's voice in her head startled her from her thoughts. How long had passed? Judging by how far the moons had progressed across the sky it had been quite a while. '*They will be alongside us shortly. Now that we are all together again, I have shown each of the other dragons an image of where we are going. If for any reason we do get separated, then we will aim to meet up at the Valley of the Griffins.*'

Kira experienced a flash of irritation that Fang had not asked her opinion before deciding to share such important information with the others. She could not fault the dragon's logic, but it was hard not to dwell on the fact that Fang had let their biggest bargaining asset go unused. Had Fang done this deliberately to test her? Her dragon was perceptive and clever. She felt sure he already knew her better than her parents had ever done. Was Fang manipulating her just as she intended to manipulate Pell? She laughed aloud at that thought.

'What a group we are!' she muttered through her chuckling.

'What's happened?' Nolita asked, leaning forwards. 'What's going on?'

'Nothing, Nolita,' Kira replied over her shoulder. 'Nothing at all.'

A sudden movement to their right drew her eyes. Firestorm and Aurora were descending into formation alongside them, their colours not distinguishable in the darkness, but their black outlines clearly different from those of night dragons.

Kira's back ached, and her eyes felt hot and gritty with tiredness. They needed to get as far from the night dragon enclave as possible under cover of darkness. If they were going to rest it would be better to do it during the daytime. But she was so exhausted that she felt it could be dangerous to continue flying. One thing was sure – no matter when they stopped, Pell would argue the case for pressing on longer.

Fang was also weary. The rhythm of his wing-beats was faster than usual as he strained to keep up with the much larger night dragon. Shadow was setting a wicked pace.

'Yet more bravado, no doubt,' Kira sighed. '*Time for you to start planting those ideas in Shadow's mind, Fang,*' she told him. '*We need to rest. Pell's probably feeling great after Firestorm's healing earlier, and Shadow had a day's rest before setting out tonight. The rest of us are beat. We need to stop, if only for a short while. Do you think we're being followed?*'

There was a pause before Fang answered. '*No,*' he said. '*At least, if there are any dragons following, they are too far behind for me to sense. I rather suspect they have given up and gone back. A break would be good. I shall see what I can do.*'

A few minutes passed in silence.

'*Kira, Shadow has just asked if any of we three "smaller" dragons, or our riders, require a rest,*' Fang eventually told her. '*How would you like me to respond?*'

Kira made a rude noise.

'*I shall interpret that as "Yes, thank you, Shadow.*

210

*That would be much appreciated,*"' Fang responded, his tone deadpan.

Kira could feel his amusement through the bond. '*You're just loving this, aren't you?*' she accused.

'*I do find it entertaining, yes,*' he admitted. '*Firestorm also had the good sense to brush off Shadow's insult. Aurora, on the other wing, is rather less pleased. Her response to Shadow's phrasing was so cold I'll be surprised if our night dragon friend is not suffering frostbite! Tell Nolita to hold on. We are going down.*'

Although the first hint of the approaching dawn was already beginning to lighten the sky to the east, it was still effectively full night. Of the dragons, Fang had by far the best night vision. For all her posturing, Shadow was sensible enough to accept this, so it was Fang who directed them down to a landing point next to a small stand of trees in the middle of a huge open field, where the land was flat in all directions.

Once safely on the ground, the riders were quick to dismount. The trees were spaced widely enough for the dragons to move underneath the leafy canopy. Camouflaging the dragons on the ground was key to avoid capture, Kira realised. It was easy enough here, but as they moved further northwards into the open tundra they would be less likely to find such convenient cover.

'Let's have a brief fire and get some hot food and drink inside us,' Kira suggested.

'A fire!' Pell challenged immediately. 'Are you mad? It'll draw the night dragons like moths.'

Kira sighed. 'You're welcome to eat cold food if you wish, Pell,' she told him. 'But I'm going to cook, whether you like it or not. It's been a challenging day and we need to eat properly. It's not a short journey to the Valley of the Griffins. We're going to need all our strength. Let's try to gather some wood.'

Elian and Nolita were quick to join Kira in her search, but Pell remained still for some moments before reluctantly making a token effort. Soon they had gathered a good pile of wood, but kindling was impossible to find.

'Nolita, can Firestorm light it for us?' Kira asked. 'It would save a lot of time and I don't want to have the fire alight any longer than necessary. We're not going to be here long enough to worry about building shelters. Our dragons can cover us with their wings while we sleep.'

Nolita looked horrified. Even in the darkness, Kira could tell that the colour had drained from the girl's face at Kira's suggestion of sleeping close to the dragons, and she looked close to tears. But somehow Nolita held herself together. Her eyes went blank for an instant as she communicated Kira's request. 'He says he will,' she replied.

'Good. Thank you, Nolita. Stand back, everyone.'

Firestorm curled his head around on his long neck until it was close to where the riders had piled the wood. The young people moved well back. Kira held her breath as the dragon inhaled. An image flashed into her mind of Firestorm's flaming breath destroying the trees in the other world. She winced, but she need not have worried. When Fire breathed out, the flame that spewed from his mouth was small and controlled, but very hot.

The gathered branches and sticks were not altogether dry. They spluttered and popped at the blaze of heat, and smoke billowed into clouds that fingered their way through the branches and leaves, curling and reaching up as if feeling for the open sky. Firestorm continued to breathe out and out, his fiery breath seemingly neverending.

'That should be enough, thank you, Nolita,' Kira said, stepping forwards.

A heartbeat later Firestorm stopped his flame and drew his head away to allow more space around the fire. Kira held her hands out towards the dancing orange tongues, enjoying the warmth and friendly light they cast. The others moved forwards to join her. Now that it was up to temperature, the smoke from the fire had reduced to little more than a haze, but the smell of it lingered under the trees for some time.

Within a very short time Kira had a pan of water heating, whilst simultaneously frying up a meaty concoction that smelled heavenly to the tired riders. Considering his reluctance to help build a fire, Pell was quick enough to dig in to his portion of the food. He ate so fast that Kira was left wondering exactly what he had been fed during his short spell in the night dragon cell. Not a lot by the look of it, she thought, a wicked little smile twisting her lips as the words 'Serves him right' crossed her mind.

'*That's not very charitable, Kira,*' Fang teased, keeping his tone as serious as ever.

'*I've just fed him, haven't I?*' she snapped. '*After his lack of appreciation for the risks we faced to get him out of that cell, and his objection to the fire, I'd say that's pretty charitable. I can't help it if he's a self-centred, arrogant little—*'

'I hardly think you could describe him as little,' Fang interrupted, clearly amused by her vitriolic response. '*He is bigger than you are.*'

'There's little and there's little,' she responded.

Fang did not understand, but he did not need to. Kira's tone said it all.

'Just remember that you are supposed to be letting him think he is leading,' Fang said. 'You forced his hand tonight with the fire. If you keep doing that sort of thing, he will become very difficult. Try to let him get his way every now and then. Perhaps you could practise. Why not thank him for suggesting the rest stop?'

'Why not?' she replied, her mental voice thick with sarcasm. 'If I choke on the words, though, would you have Elian and Nolita throw my body on the fire? I always fancied cremation over burial.'

'Just do it, Kira!'

She took a deep breath and schooled her expression before looking across at Pell, who was already finishing the last of his food.

'Thanks, Pell,' she said. The words sounded strained to her ears, but there was no sign of Pell having noticed.

'What for, Kira?' he asked, the suspicion in his voice undisguised.

'For suggesting a stop,' she replied. 'I'm exhausted.'

'Me too,' Elian added. 'I was falling asleep towards the end there. I couldn't have gone much further.'

Pell's face brightened slightly. 'No problem,' he said. 'We've all got to rest some time. The question is – how long do we rest for? It'll be light soon. I'm not sure that travelling by day is such a good idea.'

'I agree,' Kira said, trying her best to make the two words sound genuine. 'But we may have no choice. Let's face facts. It's summer. The nights are short and the days are long. We've got to try to get to the Valley of the Griffins before Segun. I'm betting he and his lieutenants are going to push hard to get there quickly. That means we're going to have to push even harder. As we go further north the nights will get progressively shorter. I can't be certain, but it's possible that there will be no night at all that far north.'

'Really?' Elian asked. 'Why's that?'

'Fang mentioned it to me some time ago, but I couldn't follow his explanation,' Kira admitted. 'Try asking Ra. And if you understand her answer, you can explain it to me. The point is we're going to have to travel by day or accept that Segun is going to get to the valley before us. How long do you think Segun will fly each day, Pell?'

'Widewing has a reputation for being a strong dragon,' he replied thoughtfully. 'Segun likes to further that reputation. He's likely to push his followers to their limits for the amusement of seeing them struggle. There is one thing in our favour, though. He isn't expecting us to be following him, so there's no real need for him to rush. I wouldn't be surprised if he pushed hard for a couple of days, but then eased off the pace when he had made his point to the others.'

'So what do you suggest?' Kira asked the question through gritted teeth.

'I'm not sure,' he replied. 'I'd like to talk it over with Shadow. Let's grab a couple of hours' sleep and then press on. A lot will depend on the riders from the enclave – if they come looking for us, and in what sort of numbers.'

Kira considered his answer and, to her surprise, was forced to concede Pell was talking good sense.

'*See? That wasn't so hard,*' Fang said, amused by her admission.

'*Don't push it!*' she warned. '*If he winds me up enough, I'll kill him. That will leave you to face Shadow. How do you fancy your chances, Fang? Could you take her on? At the moment we need Pell to get the night orb. Once that part of the quest is over, however . . .*'

Kira left the sentence hanging. Fang said nothing, his amusement dying to a cold silence. If he thought she was joking, he would laugh. But Fang could see her thoughts. He knew she was deadly serious.

## Chapter Seventeen
# A Tricky Confrontation

'*Night dragons inbound! Wake up, Pell!*'

Shadow's voice shredded Pell's dreams as effectively as her teeth would rip through a deer. For the briefest moment he was confused. Dappled light danced around him. He squinted as he cracked his eyelids open. It was morning. They were sheltering under trees. Suddenly the events of the previous evening flooded back. He had no idea how long he had slept, but it felt as if he had barely closed his eyes.

A mere instant later he was in motion, but he discovered to his chagrin that Kira was already ahead of him. The girl was scrambling onto Fang's back and the dusk dragon was moving before Pell had even begun to climb up Shadow's side. Shaking off the remnants of sleep, Pell leaped up

Shadow's foreleg and swung into the saddle.

'*How many, Shadow?*' he asked.

'*Three,*' she replied. '*They're closing fast from the southeast. I cannot be certain, but I believe they have sensed our presence.*'

'*We need to get airborne then,*' Pell said, his mind racing. '*If we can all get into the air before they reach us, we'll have the advantage of numbers.*'

A quick glance around revealed Elian settling into his saddle and Nolita scrambling up Firestorm's side. Neither would be far behind Shadow, so Pell urged his dragon forwards after Fang, who had now employed his camouflage. When Shadow emerged from under the trees there was no sign of the dusk dragon.

'Where's Fang going?' Pell asked aloud. He could faintly hear the dusk dragon's retreating wingbeats, but couldn't work out the direction from which the sound was coming.

'*I'm not sure, Pell,*' Shadow replied, sounding equally confused. '*Like you, I can hear that he is airborne, but I don't know where he is going, or what he intends.*'

'Can you tell him to come back?' Pell asked. 'It's going to be hard to put on a show of strength without him.'

There was a pause.

'Fang says he'll join us shortly,' Shadow reported. 'I think he's planning something clever, but I'm not sure what.'

'Something clever!' Pell snorted, shaking his head. 'It had better be.'

Aurora emerged from the trees beside them. Firestorm was directly behind her. Pell could see Nolita's face, white with fear, and he grimaced. But at least she had good reason to be scared this time. Three night dragons were a formidable force to contend with.

'Let's go, Shadow,' he urged.

Shadow needed little encouragement. She leaped forwards and launched into the air, taking no more than a few quick bounds and a mighty first down-stroke of her wings. As soon as Pell had settled his balance into her urgent rhythm, he glanced back to check on the others. Both Aurora and Firestorm were also airborne and climbing, though Shadow was accelerating away from them.

'Don't get too far ahead of the others, Shadow,' Pell told her. 'We don't want to get too spread out. Where are the night dragons? Can you see them yet?'

The rapidly increasing wind dried his eyes and tugged at his hair. He squinted, scanning the sky for signs of the hostile dragons.

'Yes,' she replied. 'If you look over your right

*shoulder, you will see them in our rear quarter. They are up at about five hundred spans.'*

'I've got them.'

The three black dragons were descending towards them in a menacing V formation. They were still some distance away, but had the advantage of height and speed and would soon catch up. Would they attack without negotiation? Having been declared outlaws, he and Shadow were fair targets, but what about Firestorm and Aurora? Would the night dragons attack them too? He did not see how the night dragons could justify such an act of unprovoked violence. They would be jeopardising relations with not one, but two of the other three enclaves.

*'In their eyes it is not unprovoked,'* Shadow told him. *'The night dragons will justify their actions with our outlaw status. By flying with us, Firestorm and Aurora are viewed as outlaws too. Relations between the day and night dragon enclaves have always been strained, and the dawn dragon enclave is so small it is considered unimportant.'*

'Great!' Pell muttered. *'No help there, then. Where the blazes are Fang and Kira? If we had the advantage of numbers, they might think twice.'*

Shadow did not answer. Pell could feel her reaching out with her mind, but if she received

221

any response from Fang she did not say anything.

They were well above the ground now, and climbing fast. Judging by the height of the sun above the horizon, Pell estimated it must be a couple of hours after dawn. They had slept for about four hours. Not long enough to feel totally rested, but enough to stave off the effects of severe fatigue. Despite the adrenalin burning through his body, his mind still felt fogged with the remnants of sleep.

They could not outrun the hostile night dragons. The few wispy clouds were not solid enough to offer cover and landing was out of the question. No matter how hard he tried, he could not see a way of avoiding a potentially lethal conflict.

'*The lead night dragon is telling us to land, or fight,*' Shadow said suddenly. '*What shall I tell him?*'

Pell tried to think.

'*My instinct is to tell him to go to hell, but what do the other dragons say?*' he said eventually.

'*They express similar sentiments.*'

He looked left and right. Since Shadow had slowed to allow the others to catch up, Aurora had moved up into formation to their right, and Firestorm to their left. Elian gave him a hand signal that he interpreted as 'Go ahead'.

'*Let's do it then,*' Pell growled. '*Tell them. We'll turn and meet them head to head.*'

'*Wait a moment!*' Shadow's voice sounded suddenly excited.

'*What is it? What's going on?*'

'*It's Fang,*' she said. '*He's asked me to stall them. He says he's not quite in position yet. I have no idea what he's planning, but he was taking a lot of care to make sure his message was not overheard.*'

'*All right, but they're closing fast,*' Pell replied, glancing over his shoulder again. '*Even if we try to run, it won't delay a fight for long.*'

'*If I got Fang's message right, we won't need to hold them off for long.*'

Pell's mind flashed through possible options. What in blue blazes are you doing, Kira? he wondered. If they turned now, they would at least have a reasonable chance of facing off against the night dragons. Delaying more than a few seconds would leave them unable to turn in time and vulnerable to attack from above and behind. To continue running felt like madness, but he could feel Shadow's trust and respect for Fang through the bond. Much as he hated to admit it, if he had to rely on any of his companions to get them out of a situation like this, Kira would be his natural choice. She had a cool head under pressure and nothing appeared to rattle her confidence.

'All right, Shadow,' he said decisively. 'We'll give

Fang and Kira their chance. Let's hope they know what they're doing. Drag out the chase as best you can.'

Shadow responded by entering a shallow dive to convert their height into speed. Aurora and Firestorm stayed alongside in close formation. The night dragons continued to gain, but much more slowly. Pell checked over his shoulder with frequent glances. His heart began to beat faster and faster. Their pursuers noticeably gained on them with every glance. They loomed large now, black and menacing, but it was too late to try to gain a defensive position. The night dragons were too close.

'*Get ready for a tight turn, Pell,*' Shadow warned. '*Fang says he is in position. I still don't know what he intends, but on his call we're going to split our formation. I'm to climb and turn right. The others have their directions.*'

Pell gritted his teeth. The situation galled him. They were taking orders from Kira and Fang. Shadow might sound comfortable with this, but Pell was far from happy. Suddenly he was being pressed hard into the saddle as Shadow twisted her wings to initiate a viciously sharp climbing turn. The world around him instantly took on shades of grey as he fought the physical effects of the sudden force acting down through his body. Previous experience had taught him the best thing he could do was to tense all the muscles in his legs and stomach as hard as he could. He growled as he did so, using his anger to strengthen his straining manoeuvre.

His colour vision returned and his head swam as Shadow snapped out of the turn. Bright golden dots of light swarmed at the edges of his vision, but Pell ignored them. More pressing was the night dragon that had turned above them. It was the leader. Its talons gleamed hard and deadly. Pell shuddered, imagining what it would feel like to be caught in their grip. Why was Shadow not weaving? Surely it would be better to keep turning if they were to make it difficult for their attacker? The night dragon could fold its wings and attack them at any second.

'*Desist from your attack. Land now, or your leader dies!*'

Pell could not quite believe what he was hearing.

'*Not my words, but Fang's,*' Shadow informed him. '*I'm relaying what he is telling them.*'

Another glance up at the lead night dragon and Pell could sense its confusion. Just above it, but angling away was a smaller dragon. It was Fang. Somehow he had managed to snatch the night dragon's rider from his saddle. He had then shed his camouflage and was now angling away, with the night dragonrider squirming in his grip.

'How?' Pell asked.

'Apparently Fang is learning some new hunting tricks from Kira,' Shadow chuckled. 'At Kira's insistence, Fang put all his effort into gaining as much height as possible. She anticipated our direction of flight based on where the night dragons were coming from and our planned destination. As we set off, the night dragons gave chase. Fang kept climbing hard, watching as we passed underneath him and waiting until the night dragons committed to their final attacking descent.'

'Then Fang dropped in on top of them,' Pell finished. 'Clever. She used us like bait to draw them in and pounced when all their attention was focused on us.'

He looked around. The three night dragons were circling now. There was obvious confusion. The two riders were signalling to one another. Pell could not see them well enough to make out their gestures at this range, but he could guess what they meant. He grinned as he thought how they must be feeling.

The riderless dragon began keening; a high-pitched screech that set Pell's teeth on edge and sent shivers down his spine.

'Fang has repeated his order for them to land.' Shadow sounded smug now. 'I think they realise they have little choice. They are complying.'

She was right, Pell realised. The three black dragons were descending past them in a tight spiral, the lead dragon still emitting the tortured scream that was making his ears itch to be plugged.

'Why is the lead dragon making that horrible noise?' Pell asked silently. 'I've never heard a dragon make such an awful racket before.'

'Her rider is injured,' Shadow explained. 'She can feel his pain. I think he has a broken ankle. Fang says the rider's foot got tangled in his stirrup as he was snatched from the saddle. Fang pulled him free, breaking his ankle in the process. He was lucky not to lose his foot altogether.'

'Ouch!' Pell winced, unconsciously loosening his own feet in his stirrups. 'That's got to hurt! I can't say I feel much sympathy, but I wouldn't like to be in his boots right now. Has Fang given them any further instructions?'

'No. Not yet.'

'Then let's suggest we order them to stay where they are until midday,' Pell said thoughtfully. 'We can tell the dragons that we'll drop their rider somewhere northwest of here, but they're not to begin searching for him until this afternoon. We can say that if we sense them following us early, we'll kill him.'

Pell put as much conviction into the threat as he could, knowing full well that Shadow was a terrible liar. If she knew he would not follow through with his threat, she would not be convincing. Shadow relayed the message and, to Pell's surprise, Fang was quick to implement his idea.

Moments later the others had slipped into formation with Shadow leading the way, while the night dragons continued to spiral downwards. Looking back, Pell saw them land. It was impossible to tell if the night dragonriders would keep their dragons on the ground until midday, but he felt the warmth of victory spread through him as the shapes of the night dragons dwindled into the distance. The only niggling cold spot was a hard, knotty fact that nestled deep in his gut: the victory was not really his. It belonged to Kira and Fang.

## Chapter Eighteen
# Questions, Questions

'Hold him down!' Elian ordered firmly. 'Sit on him. Do whatever you have to, but keep him still. This is going to hurt.'

Pell pushed the rider to the ground and sat on his chest, pinning the man's arms against his sides. Kira leaned her full weight across the rider's thighs and pressed down with all her might against his knees with her forearms. Nolita kept his head down, cupping his forehead with her palms.

'What are you doing to me?' he yelled, panic lending him extraordinary strength as he struggled against the three young dragonriders. 'Let me go!'

'I'm going to set your ankle,' Elian told him, keeping his voice calm. 'Not even a day dragon's healing breath will help you unless we get the bones in the right place first.'

'I don't want that day dragon anywhere near me,' the man gasped. 'Leave me alone. Get off! AAAArrrrrgggh!'

The rider twisted and writhed as Elian rolled up the man's trouser leg and began to gently pull at the boot that concealed his damaged ankle. There was a horrible sucking, squelching sound as the boot began to work loose. A small flood of blood poured from the top as the foot started to come free.

'KEEP HIM STILL!'

'Easier said than done,' Pell grunted, fighting hard to keep the man from twisting out from under him.

'Ooohhh! That's not pretty!' Elian observed, cringing as he finally freed the foot and put the boot aside. 'The bone isn't just broken. It's sticking out through his skin!'

He grabbed his water bottle and emptied the contents over the wound to wash away the surface blood. The rider's body bucked like a wild horse as the stream of water triggered a new wave of pain. Elian felt sick. A glance up at Kira revealed that she had her eyes shut. Her skin looked suspiciously pale. Pell sat on the man's chest, facing the other way, his body shielding Nolita's view. The gruesome task of trying to set the bone fell to Elian. Why do I get all the messy jobs? he wondered. He lifted his water bottle to his lips and let the last few drops dribble into his mouth before putting it to one side.

'All right. Here goes,' he warned.

The grating sound of bone on bone as he pulled and twisted the foot in an effort to realign the ankle was almost drowned out by the man's screams. Almost. What he could not hear, however, he could feel. His stomach turned as he fought to get the bones in line. Suddenly the screams stopped as the man lost consciousness. Elian grunted and gave one final twisting pull. The ankle looked straight, but it was so swollen that it was difficult to tell. It was as good as he could get it.

'Nolita,' he gasped, wiping the cold sweat from his forehead with his sleeve. His hands were slick with blood. 'Could you ask Firestorm to do his stuff now? I don't think we need to hold him down any more, Pell. He looks unlikely to wake up for a while. Let's stand back and see what miracles Fire can work.'

Nolita, Pell and Kira were all quick to move away from the unconscious body of the rider, who looked deathly pale against the lush green grass. Elian realised he had neglected to check whether the rider was still breathing. A man could die of shock under circumstances like these.

Too late to worry about that now, Elian thought, as Firestorm lowered his head and drew in a deep breath.

Elian did not really want to watch, but he could not help himself. He found the blue nimbus of the day dragon's healing fire mesmerising. Even though he had seen the miraculous healing effects of Firestorm's fiery breath before, he realised he was holding his breath as the day dragon breathed his fire across the rider's leg.

'Breathe,' he told himself. As he inhaled he noticed a faint scent in the air. It was sweet, like that of a flower, but with a nutty, woody edge. He had not noticed it before. Perhaps during previous healings a breeze had carried the smell away, or maybe he had simply been too caught up in the moment. He closed his eyes and drew in a deep breath. A feeling of healthy energy rushed through him. It was a heady experience.

Even though his eyes were still closed, Elian knew the moment Firestorm stopped breathing out the healing flames. For a moment he had almost felt bonded to the day dragon. It was strange. He was bonded to Aurora, yet he had felt a connection with the day dragon.

'*Did you feel that, Ra?*' he asked uncertainly.

'*Feel what?*' she asked.

'Oh, nothing,' Elian said quickly. 'It was probably my imagination running away with itself.'

'Sounds intriguing. What did you imagine?'

'Well, this might sound crazy, Ra, but I could've sworn that I saw inside Fire's mind while he was healing the rider. It was almost as if we were bonded, but the link didn't feel like ours.'

'That's not crazy at all,' she replied. 'A day dragon risks much when he heals, for at that moment his mind is vulnerable. If another dragon were to look into his mind during that moment of weakness, Firestorm would not be able to conceal even his deepest secrets. Our bond is strengthening your mind. Your mental voice has much more power now than when we first met. It does not surprise me that you were able to reach out to Firestorm when he was at his most open. The scent of the healing fire probably acted as a conduit.'

'The scent of his fire? Why would that serve to link our minds?'

'All the senses work in harmony, Elian,' the dragon said sagely. 'Quite how our brains work is a mystery. Our senses trigger mental responses rather like reflexes. It's not impossible that the smell of the healing fire triggered your mind to reach out. Don't worry about it. Nothing can replace our bond.'

'That's good to know.'

Firestorm stepped back from the unconscious

rider and Elian checked the man's ankle. It looked completely normal now and the man's breathing was deep and regular. He looked relaxed and free from pain.

Although it was soaked with blood, Elian put the man's sock and boot back onto his freshly healed foot. There was no telling how long the man would sleep for. Ra insisted the man's dragon would locate him easily by following the pull of their bond, but Elian did not want to take any chances. By night it would be bitterly cold. They did not want him to lose his foot to frostbite because they had not wrapped it.

The others were in their respective saddles by the time he had finished.

'Come on, Elian!' Pell urged, his voice loud and commanding. 'We haven't got all day.'

Elian looked around one last time before leaping up Ra's foreleg and swinging into his saddle. The man was lying on top of a small grassy mound, with a stream nearby, so he would not be short of water when he awoke. There were occasional trees along the bank of the stream, but no woodland for some distance.

'*He looks very vulnerable there,*' Elian observed to Ra as they launched again. '*Are there any predators in this part of Areth?*'

'There are predators in every region of Areth,' Ra replied gravely. 'But I don't sense anything in the immediate vicinity. To be honest I will be surprised if the night dragons wait until midday before following. Don't worry, Elian. He will not be there for long.'

'This quest is getting more dangerous by the day, isn't it?'

'I never promised you an easy ride, Elian, but don't you feel it's better this way? If our task had been to simply fly somewhere, pick up an orb and return it to the Oracle, what sort of a life purpose would that be? The adventure of life is in the journey, not the destination. Death is the inevitable end for everyone – man and dragon. Without danger on the way, there is little adventure. I admit we have already encountered times when a little less danger would have been welcome, but I am not complaining. I feel alive, Elian. I feel needed. Important. Can you feel it too?'

Elian knew exactly what Aurora meant. He had always dreamed of adventure, but the more gruesome elements that went along with danger had never featured in his imagination. It was just as well that his parents didn't know what he was doing. Excitement and adventure was one thing, but if they knew the sort of perils he was facing, they would worry themselves into an early grave.

The wind felt good in Elian's hair as they

climbed. He breathed deeply, enjoying the taste of the clean, cold air and banishing thoughts of danger to the very back of his mind. Flying was so exhilarating. It was a feeling like no other: liberating, exciting and at times deeply spiritual. His bond with Ra made it more so, for without that meeting of minds, riding her might be like riding on the back of any other animal. The excitement of flying would be there, but it was the bond that made the experience really special.

The landscape had changed drastically from the spectacular peaks of the great central mountain range. Those gigantic rocky heads had faded into the distance and were now little more than purple hints on the horizon behind them. Ahead the terrain was flat and green, although in winter this entire region would be buried in snow.

Such a scene was hard for Elian to imagine. Even in the depths of the cold season at his home in Racafi the temperature did not drop low enough for snow to fall. In the last two weeks he had seen snowy peaks on three mountain ranges. It looked beautiful; so pure and white. He wondered what it would feel like to touch. They were heading towards more mountains to find the home of the griffins. Maybe he would get the chance to touch it there.

During the next three days the four dragons carried their riders a vast distance, flying from early in the morning until late in the evening. The weather held fair. Light winds and sparse cloud helped their progress, but each day took its toll. The riders slept little and rose weary each morning. The breaks they took felt shorter with each stop. They saw no cities, or even towns. The land was harsh and forbidding, with little to offer settlers. They did pass over a few small clusters of dwellings and Elian wondered what had possessed the inhabitants to set up home in the middle of nowhere.

They stopped briefly at one such settlement late in the morning of the second day. Food was not a problem as the dragons were happy to hunt, but the four riders were getting sick of eating nothing but meat. Shadow obligingly killed an extra deer, which they traded at the tiny village for some fresh vegetables and bread.

'Have you seen any other dragons passing this way recently?' Elian asked as he helped a villager hang the carcass of the deer up on a hook to be butchered.

The man shook his head immediately. 'No,' he said. 'Don't see many dragons out this way. You're the first riders we've seen these last three seasons, or more.'

On the one hand Elian was pleased they were not following directly in Segun's wake, but on the other, it meant they had no idea if they had overtaken him on the quest.

Kira and Pell continued to clash regularly, but their disagreements appeared to be losing their fire. The two bickered over trivialities, but Elian noticed that Kira often provoked such confrontations to subtly deflect Pell from arguments over bigger issues. The Racafian girl was devilishly clever. She was letting Pell feel he was leading, but all along she had him dancing to her tune and he could not see it. If the older boy realised what she was doing, Elian knew tempers would flare spectacularly. It seemed to fall to him to mediate – not a role he relished, but one he knew was essential if they were to see this quest through to the end.

Nolita was little better. She did not argue like Kira and Pell, but it was clear she was still having a hard time coming to terms with being a dragonrider. She continued to face up to her fears, but the constant stress was taking a heavy toll. The blond girl had been thin and undernourished when Elian and Kira had first met her in Cemaria. Although she ate a healthy amount of food each day, Nolita continued to look gaunt, with no physical signs of improvement in her health.

Every time they stopped to rest, Nolita raced off to the nearest water to wash her hands. It was a part of who Nolita was. But a worrying string of other little rituals was now building up. She had developed an after-landing ritual, a pre-food ritual, a post-food ritual, a pre-launch ritual, a pre-bedtime ritual and a start-of-the-day ritual. At each of these times, Nolita ran through a set routine of actions in a particular order. If any of the patterns were interrupted, she became flustered.

Nolita rarely spoke to the others, even when they tried to include her in conversations. With Pell and Kira intent on power games, there were times when Elian felt as isolated as Nolita. At least he enjoyed the company of his dragon. He knew Nolita could not even do that.

What had possessed the Oracle to place its life in the hands of such a dysfunctional group? Elian wondered. But despite their differences, he could see a certain method in the Oracle's choices. Each rider and dragon pairing had different, but identifiable, strengths. Nolita and Firestorm were brave. Pell and Shadow were strong and ambitious. Kira and Fang were clever and tenacious. What qualities did he and Ra bring to the group? Ra was special. He smiled as his thoughts drifted and his eyes automatically sought out his beautiful golden

dragon. What had he and Ra been chosen for . . . ?
It was a question that worried him often. If each
rider and dragon partnership had been chosen for a
particular quality required, what were he and Ra
supposed to be good at?

## Chapter Nineteen
# An Unexpected Delay

'M-m-more mountains,' Kira grumbled, her mouth struggling to formulate the words. The cold had taken her beyond shivering some time ago. She growled at her dragon through clenched teeth. 'What is it with d-d-dragons and m-mountains anyway?'

'*Mountains make good homes, Kira,*' Fang replied, his voice in her mind sounding perplexed. '*They are beautiful, majestic and proud, yet they also offer challenges, excitement, and sometimes danger. You humans choose to live in such boring places. You miss so much.*'

'The savannah lands of Racafi are beautiful! They're also wild and dangerous,' Kira snapped, a surge of passion and anger cutting through her torpor for a moment, allowing her to speak more clearly. 'It's you d-dragons who're m-m-misguided. I was n-never bored in Racafi. M-more importantly it was w-w-warm. I'm b-beginning to f-feel as if I'll never be w-warm again.'

The air was smooth, but very cold, as they flew over the foothills. This was just as well, as Kira was not holding on to anything. She had her arms folded across her chest and was rubbing the outside of her arms in an attempt to generate heat.

She had lost all feeling in the tip of her nose, and her ears burned with the cold, despite being tucked under the lined flaps of her hat. She wriggled her toes in her boots, but they were numb beyond feeling and her fingers ached inside her gloves. They would have to land.

'I'll admit the temperature where you lived was rather pleasant,' Fang agreed. 'But it made me feel lazy and listless. Nice for a change maybe, but not as a place to live. In the mountains it is easy to feel alive and full of vitality.'

'It sounds as if we're going to have a problem when this quest is over, Fang,' Kira replied, switching to mental communication to save her aching jaw. 'If you think you're going to convince me to live with you in some cave in the mountains, you'd better think again. Can you tell the others to look for a place to land, please? I don't care what Pell says, I need to sit near a fire and warm up. I'm frozen. Look. There's some woodland over there. Let's land near the edge.'

There was a slight pause. 'I've spoken with the others,' Fang announced. 'Shadow is not happy. She and Pell want to press on to the Valley of the Griffins with all haste.'

'No surprises there then!' Kira found it hard to believe the others were faring any better than she was, but then again maybe they were. Elian had lived on a high plateau and Nolita came from a climate that was generally colder than that of Racafi. From what she understood, Pell would be in his element here. Kira did not know, and did not care to know, much about his background. However, it was clear that he had lived near the foothills of a mountain range in Central Isaa. 'Tell him it's an emergency,' she said. 'Tell him whatever you like. Just get them to land.'

'All right, Kira. Hold on. We're going down.'

Fang waited until he knew Kira was holding onto the pommel grips and then he folded his wings and dipped into a steep descent. They swooped down and landed next to the woods that Kira had pointed out. Moments later the other three dragons were landing around them.

Kira was a tangle of limbs as she tried to dismount. It was embarrassing, but her body refused to respond properly and she slid, out of control, down

Fang's side. The thump as she landed jarred through her body, winding her. Time blurred. It seemed that no sooner had she registered the shock of the impact than Elian was there. He helped her to her feet and supported her with an arm around her back, talking to her in a low, comforting voice. Fang's voice was there in her mind as well, apologetic and concerned. She suddenly realised she had no idea what either of them was saying. Their voices were echoing and overlapping in a confusing barrage of noise. Nothing made any sense. All she could discern was that they were worried about something.

Now that she was on the ground, Kira felt warm – warm and tired. She started to fumble at her jacket in an effort to remove it, but someone stopped her. A flash of anger sparked. Why didn't they leave her alone? They'd landed now. What did it matter to anyone if she used the time to rest?

The rim of a cup was placed against her lips. The contents were warm and sweet. It tasted heavenly. Where had that come from? Was that the crackle of a fire? Her eyelids felt so heavy, but the warmth of the drink as it slipped down her throat was wonderful. She reached up to the cup, trying to tip it in an effort to drink faster. This too was denied.

'Don't take it away!' she mumbled. 'More.'

The cup was placed against her lips again and

again, but the person controlling the cup only allowed her small sips. She wanted to cry out against the restriction, but found that the warm, dark tunnel of sleep offered the easier path.

It was the tone of Pell's voice that brought back her focus. He sounded frustrated and annoyed, and she knew instinctively that she was the source of both emotions. The corners of her mouth tweaked up into a smile. It felt good to have such power that she could annoy him without even trying. She cracked her eyes open just wide enough to see. How long had she slept? It was still light, but the sun looked as if it was sinking into the west.

'You've been a rider longer than any of us. Don't tell me you've never flown too high, or for too long in cold air. It takes quite a while to recover. You must know that. I did it on my first day with Ra, and it nearly got both of us killed. It looks as though Kira pushed even further than I did. I say we give her as long as she needs.'

That's fighting talk coming from Elian, Kira thought. He seemed so soft and easy-going. It was good to see him standing his ground. There was a noticeable silence. Pell wasn't rushing to answer him. Elian had struck home with that comment. Kira tucked away the thought for future reference and carried on listening.

'Very well,' Pell sighed. 'We will leave for the Valley of the Griffins first thing in the morning.'

'Have either of you ever seen a griffin?' Nolita asked, her voice sounding small and pathetic. 'It's just that I was wondering how big they are.'

Kira surreptitiously opened her eyes a crack further to try to see how the boys reacted. She had never seen a griffin, though she knew from stories they were reputed to be half lion and half eagle. How a creature like that had come into existence was difficult to imagine, but the dragons were confident they were real and that they lived in these mountains. The dragons were rarely wrong.

'No, I've never seen one, Nolita,' Elian replied.

'Me neither,' Pell added.

There was a slight pause. 'Ra tells me they're similar in size to a small horse, but not to mention horses in their presence,' Elian said. 'Apparently they hate horses. She also tells me that they don't originate from this world, but from the world on the other side of the gateways.'

'How does she know that?' Pell asked, sounding dubious.

'She says the story goes back many years to one of the most famous quests in the dawn dragon archives. Aside from the Great Quest, it was the only one known to involve several dragons. The

Oracle gave them the joint task of bringing many strange and dangerous creatures from the other world to Areth. It seems the men there were hunting these creatures to extinction.'

'Why did the Oracle care?' Nolita asked, her voice distinctly shaky. 'And if they're dangerous, why bring them to our world?'

'Ra says she doesn't know for sure, but thinks the Oracle foresaw something in the future of Areth that involved these creatures. It was a long and dangerous adventure for both the dragons and their riders. Many of the creatures were hostile to the idea of changing worlds, but somehow they were convinced to come. Apparently there were not many of them, so Ra doubts they will ever present much of a problem to the people of Areth. I shouldn't worry too much, Nolita. The creatures all live in remote regions of our world and, from what little I've seen of the other world, I'd say they're far better off here.'

'So there won't be many of these griffins, then,' Nolita said thankfully. 'That's good.'

'Well, Ra doesn't think so. Only a handful came through the gateway, but that was a very long time ago and no one has had much contact with them since. She tells me the griffins are fiercely territorial. They are also known for their strength and bravery.

The story hinted that they may have brought some great treasure from the other world that they now guard jealously.'

'Could that treasure be the night orb?' Pell asked suddenly. 'That would make sense, wouldn't it? The Oracle sends us to "seek brave ones' counsel". The brave ones are guarding something precious. Maybe that something is the very thing that the Oracle needs to survive. Perhaps our task is to take it from them.'

Kira nearly laughed aloud. Pell was so predictable, and his thinking so single track. This could cause a problem, though. Now that he had the treasure idea in his head, changing his perspective would be all but impossible. It was like his idea to go to the night dragon enclave all over again.

Elian was shaking his head. 'I don't think so, Pell,' he said. 'That doesn't sound right to me. If the Oracle wanted us to take something from the griffins, surely this would have been hinted at in the rhyme. Listen: *Release the dark orb – death brings me life. Take brave ones' counsel, 'ware ye the knife. Exercise caution, stay pure and heed, Yield unto justice: truth will succeed.*'

'But it *does* hint at that,' Pell insisted. '*Release the dark orb – death brings me life.* We have to release the dark orb from the griffins. We may need to kill some of them to get it. That's not too hard to see, is it?'

Brilliant! thought Kira. It'll take a lightning bolt from heaven to turn him now.

'But what about the rest of the verse?' Elian responded quickly. 'Your interpretation doesn't fit the last two lines at all.'

'They could mean anything,' Pell said dismissively. 'You said yourself that the verse about the first orb didn't make sense until Firestorm and Nolita had actually got it. I'll bet this one will be the same.'

'That's something we can agree on,' Elian muttered. 'Look, I'm not trying to kill your enthusiasm, Pell,' he continued at a more normal volume, clearly trying to sound reasonable. 'I just want you to keep an open mind, that's all. Stealing isn't *staying pure* or *truthful*. The last two lines of the Oracle's verse mentions both of these. And *exercise caution* sounds like good advice right now.'

'The orbs are dragon orbs, aren't they?' Nolita asked, deflecting whatever response Pell might have made.

'Yes,' the boys said together.

'Well we know that dragons don't exist in the other world, so why would there be a dragon orb there for the griffins to bring through?' she went on.

Brilliant! Kira thought again, this time without the sarcasm. Nolita, you're a genius! Pell can't answer that.

But she was wrong.

'Maybe the orb had been taken there on a previous quest,' Pell suggested thoughtfully. 'The Oracle has been around for millennia. Who's to say that it didn't send the orb to the other world in the first place? Maybe it was for safekeeping, or something.'

Kira groaned silently. If he was willing to clutch at such long straws, then he was totally sold on his idea. It was time to break up the conversation. It had been interesting, but it was no longer going anywhere. She faked a yawn and stretched out in catlike fashion. Elian was by her side in a flash.

'Are you all right, Kira?' he asked. 'Are you warm enough?'

'I'm fine, thanks,' she said sleepily. 'What time is it?'

'Late afternoon. You slept most of the day,' Pell said.

He might just as well have said 'wasted most of the day' with that tone, Kira thought. She decided not to rise to the bait. He might want a fight, but she was not ready to give him one today.

'No wonder I feel good,' she said, keeping her

250

voice deliberately distant and content. 'Where are we?'

'Not far from the Valley of the Griffins,' Pell grumbled.

'Take no notice of him,' Elian told her. 'We'll get there early tomorrow. The griffins are unlikely to go anywhere.'

'No, but Segun is,' Pell said pointedly. 'If he's beaten us to the orb, getting it back will not be easy. I'd rather take on some griffins than Segun and the other senior night dragonriders any day.'

Much as Kira hated to admit it, Pell did have a good point. She opened her eyes fully and turned to look at the white outlines of the mountains. The snowline extended almost to their bases. She shivered at the sight. If Segun had beaten them to the orb because of her failure to cope with the cold, then two things were sure: Pell would never forgive her and the quest would become more difficult than ever.

## Chapter Twenty
# Valley of the Griffins

'*Does Fang really know where he's going, Shadow? Or is he making this up as he goes along? It feels as if we're going in circles. I'm sure we've been along this valley before.*'

'*Fang assures me it is not far now,*' Shadow replied, but her voice in Pell's mind held a hint of uncertainty.

They had been flying for most of the morning. In all that time they had seen no living creature other than a solitary eagle soaring high above them in the late morning sun. It was bitterly cold up in the mountain passes. The glare of the sunlight reflecting from the great expanses of pure white snow on all sides was giving him a headache, but he was not about to complain. The weather was still holding fair. Considering how much time they had spent in mountainous terrain recently, the elements had been most kind.

'Not far is one thing, but knowing in which direction would be useful,' Pell growled aloud. This was getting ridiculous.

'*He says the entrance is not immediately obvious*,' Shadow told him. '*The griffins chose their home deliberately to avoid being found. Fang has been there once before, but it was a long time ago. He says he will recognise the signs when he sees them.*'

'A long time ago? How long is long?'

'*Around three centuries*,' Shadow admitted.

'Three centuries!' Pell breathed aloud. '*It's no wonder he's lost!*'

'*He's not lost, Pell.*' The night dragon hesitated for just a moment. '*Or at least if he is lost, then so is Segun. Look.*'

Six night dragons were flying along the valley some distance in front of them in two tandem V formations of three. The others had noticed them too. Kira and Elian were waving at him and pointing. Nolita was staring straight ahead, as she often did, but from the tilt of her body and the angle of her head it was obvious she had also spied the dark dragons.

Fortunately, Segun and his lieutenants were flying away from them, so it was unlikely that they would notice the four dragons following in their wake. Pell instinctively glanced over each shoulder in quick succession, checking the sky behind him for potential trouble. There were at least three other night dragons out there somewhere, and after the long delay of the previous day, they could easily catch up.

'We'd better slow down, Shadow. We don't want to get too close,' Pell suggested. 'I don't understand why they're flying so slowly.'

'As I said, the entrance to the Valley of the Griffins is close,' Shadow replied. 'It is not easy to see. Segun and Widewing seem to know this. Fang tells me he can see the markers that guide the way to the entrance now. The night dragons are almost on top of them. Yes. Look. They are turning.'

It was true. The night dragons turned to the right and switched formation until all six were flying in a single line, each astern and slightly below the one in front. Pell held his breath. It would only need one of them to look back up the valley, and the Oracle's chosen team would lose the element of surprise. To his amazement, it did not happen. Instead, the night dragons disappeared one by one, seemingly straight into a solid, vertical rock wall. He let out a sigh of relief.

'I don't understand,' he said. 'Why didn't they notice

us? You sensed those other night dragons while they were still miles away the other day.'

'Yes, but we were on the lookout for other dragons,' Shadow replied. 'Segun and his men have no reason to expect us to be behind them. They think you are safely locked up at the enclave and that the others have gone to Racafi. Also, the entrance to the Valley of the Griffins is rather special. I imagine their attention was very much on where they were going.'

'Special? In what way?'

'You will see,' Shadow said cryptically. 'I don't want to ruin it for you.'

Curious as Pell was, a rising feeling of panic began to take over. His relief at not having been seen by the leaders of the night dragon enclave had momentarily blinded him to the fact that Segun had beaten them to the valley. What should they do now?

The night dragons outnumbered them. Fang, Firestorm and Aurora had some interesting abilities, but for all their clever tricks he could not imagine any of them seriously troubling the night dragons if it came to a fight.

'I feel your concern,' Shadow said. 'There is no need to worry just yet, Pell. Fang tells me the night dragons will not harm us while we're in the Valley of the Griffins. We should follow Segun with all haste to ensure he does not secure the orb before we get there.'

Pell was dubious. 'And how does Fang know this?' he asked.

'He says the griffins control what happens within their valley. They will not allow an unprovoked attack. He sounds very sure. Although griffins are smaller than dragons, they are very fierce when aroused. Even Segun will be wary of angering them.'

Shadow led the way to where the night dragons had turned right and disappeared. Pell looked with growing confusion at the sheer cliff that formed the wall of the valley to his right. It looked solid. He could have sworn the night dragons had turned here, but perhaps he was mistaken. They must have turned further along the valley. A feeling of amusement filtered through the bond.

'You were not mistaken, Pell,' Shadow told him as she dipped her right wing and started to turn towards the cliff-face. 'The entrance to the valley is right here. The griffins are highly intelligent creatures and they have used a clever mix of reflected light and shadow to hide the path to their home. Only those who know the markers are likely to find it. But it's not easy to see, even when you know what you're looking for.'

They continued to turn until they were flying straight towards the solid wall of rock.

'Shadow? What are you doing, Shadow?' Pell asked aloud, a note of panic in his voice.

She did not answer. They were rapidly approaching the cliff-face and alarm bells began to ring in Pell's head. He instinctively tightened his grip on the pommel and all his muscles became taut with anticipation. Although he had learned to trust Shadow over the past two season rotations, every synapse in his brain was screaming 'DANGER!' as his sense of self-preservation kicked into full alert.

'SHADOW!'

It was too late. Even if they turned hard now, they would still hit the rock. Pell took a sharp intake of breath and closed his eyes, ducking down behind Shadow's ridge and bracing against the inevitable impact.

He counted down in his head: three, two, one . . . he flinched. Nothing happened. They should have hit the wall by now. His mind spun with confusion. He cracked his eyes open just a touch and gasped in amazement. They were flying along a narrow path, barely wider than Shadow's wingspan. He looked around and the illusion created by the colouring and texture of the cliff-face became obvious. Once penetrated, the path into the rock wall was clear, but when viewed from the valley it had been impossible to see.

The path was actually a short tunnel, open at both ends. They were already approaching the real rock wall at the far end of the short passage. Pell could just see that there was an opening to the left. It would be a tight turn for a dragon the size of Shadow, but she did not seem concerned.

'*Hang on, Pell,*' she warned.

One moment they were flying straight and level, the next Shadow's left wingtip was pointing directly at the rocky ground and the force pushing Pell into the saddle increased rapidly until he felt as though he was being crushed. Then she rolled the other way and Pell had to hang on for all he was worth to avoid sliding over Shadow's side.

He looked back over his shoulder. Kira and Fang were close behind, with Firestorm just coming into view behind them. The thought that Kira might have been close enough to see him cowering in his saddle as they approached the cliff-wall crossed his mind.

'Damn!' he muttered. 'She's not going to let me hear the last of this.'

He switched his focus forwards, grinding his teeth and screwing his face up to try to disperse the flush of embarrassment that burned his cheeks. Ahead, a rapidly widening canyon with sheer rocky walls curved away to the right. He looked up, trying to assess if it was possible to fly into this valley from above. A dragon could do it easily, but whether a rider would survive a flight in the freezing temperature up at that altitude was questionable. The mountains were not as high as those that housed the night dragon enclave, but they were high enough to offer similar dangers to the unwary.

The canyon continued to curve and widen until they emerged into the main valley. The basin here was wide and white with snow, contrasted only by the occasional grey sides of large rocks scattered across the valley floor, and the great grey cliffs powering up thousands of spans on either side. The winding line of a stream was visible in the middle of the valley, but at points where the flow slowed, the surface had frozen and the ice was hidden underneath a blanket of snow.

The six night dragons had landed not far ahead, their huge bodies standing out like dirty black scars in the skin of white snow that covered the smooth valley floor. The riders had dismounted and were standing in a huddle, surrounded by their dragons. Of the griffins, there was no sign.

Segun and his riders were quick to spot the incoming dragons. The huddle broke instantly, the dragonriders scattering to their dragons. It was too late to avoid a confrontation now. The only advantage they held over the six night dragons was one of energy, but in his heart Pell knew that a fight with Segun and his riders could only end one way – in disaster.

'*Is this definitely the place, Shadow?*' he asked quickly.

'*Yes,*' she replied confidently.

'*Then take us down,*' he ordered. '*Land us short of Segun's party. Let's not give them the wrong idea. We don't want to start a fight we can't win.*'

'*Very well, Pell,*' Shadow answered. Her voice held a hint of disappointment. She was itching to exact revenge for Segun's actions at the night dragon enclave, but she did as he asked. Spilling the lift from her wings, she entered a dramatic diving descent before swooping to an immaculate landing some one hundred paces short of the circle of night dragons. Fang, Firestorm and Aurora landed in a neat sequence beside her.

Pell looked around at his companions. Kira did not look happy, but that was to be expected. Kira was never happy with his decisions. Elian looked nervous – again understandable. Nolita's expression, however, was totally unreadable. The girl remained an enigma. He still considered her cowardly, but he knew there must be more to her than met the eye, or she would not have retrieved the first orb.

With a confidence he did not feel, Pell flipped his right leg over to meet his left and dismounted, sliding down Shadow's side and landing with a soft crump, ankle deep in snow. He walked in front of Shadow, the soft snow scrunching under his feet. It was a sound that sparked memories of his younger, boyhood years, but he knew this was no time for nostalgia. Kira, Elian and Nolita strode to meet him.

'Have you got any idea what you're doing?' Kira asked in a low voice as she approached.

Pell flashed her his most confident grin. 'None whatsoever,' he said. 'Next question?'

'What do we do now?' Elian asked, glancing ahead to where Segun and his riders were regrouping. Pell's initial gambit had proved successful in avoiding an immediate conflict. The night dragonriders had not launched straight into an attack, but Elian could not help wondering if his ploy had merely staved off the inevitable – and if so, by how long?

'We parley,' Pell replied quickly. 'Segun will be surprised to see me here. Widewing will have recognised Shadow by now, even if Segun can't identify me from this distance. We want to avoid a fight, if we can. Even if we'd used our advantage of height and energy when we first entered the valley, at best we'd have taken casualties. A more likely outcome would have seen us all dead in the snow. Our best hope is to keep them talking until the griffins decide to show themselves, or things may turn ugly.'

'That's the most sense I've heard you speak since we first met,' Elian conceded. He glanced at Kira, whose lips were pressed together in a tight line. 'What're you thinking, Kira? Do you have a better plan?'

'No,' she admitted. 'But try to keep them at a distance when we talk. They're six grown men with weapons. Don't try anything clever, Pell. We're as much at a disadvantage on the ground as we are in the air.'

Pell nodded.

The six night dragonriders were advancing towards them side by side in an ominous line. Even more menacing were their dragons, following behind.

'Let's go,' Pell said, turning to face Segun and his men. Elian moved to Pell's left, with Nolita outside him. Kira stepped into position on Pell's right and together they marched forwards as one to meet with the enemy.

## Chapter Twenty-One
# The Challenge

When the two lines of riders stopped to face off at about ten paces apart, Elian was instantly reminded of his confrontation with the bullies Borkas and Farrel on the heath near his home. At that time, he had just met with Aurora and had used his newfound friendship with the dragon to surprise the boys. He had felt strong, powerful and totally in control. He wished he could feel the same confidence now, but this time he had no secret advantages to spring on the more powerful adversaries. Neither did any of his companions.

He glanced across at Pell and Kira. They looked incredibly at ease, given the circumstances. A quick look at Nolita revealed that she, at least, looked as nervous as he felt. Her eyes, however, were not on the night dragonriders, but on the huge black dragons coming behind them. A slight movement in the corner of his eye drew Elian's attention. Taking care not to move his head, he flicked a lightning glance up and to the right before returning his focus to the line of riders ahead of them. Something was coming.

'*Ra?*' he asked silently.

'*Yes, Elian, it is a griffin,*' Ra replied, confirming his suspicion. '*As far as I can tell the night dragons are not aware of it yet.*'

'It seems I underestimated you, Pell.' Segun's voice was controlled, but his ice-blue eyes were colder than the snow that filled the valley. 'I don't know how you got here, but I'm not going to allow you to go any further. The Great Quest ends right here, right now.'

'No, Segun,' Pell replied. 'I've not come this far to fail. Neither have my companions. We intend to see it through to the end.'

'Which is as it should be,' cried a harsh voice from above.

As one, the five night dragonriders around Segun reached instinctively for weapons as they looked up in alarm. Only Segun of the six did not flinch. Elian was pleased to note that Pell and Kira did not give so much as a flicker of emotion at the arrival of the griffin. The four younger riders stood their ground, staring straight at Segun, as the fantastic creature descended vertically to land gently between the two parties of riders and dragons. It folded its wings against its sides and circled once before stopping directly between Pell and Segun.

Elian could see out of the corner of his eye that Nolita was almost as pale as the snow around her, but she did not move a muscle. Good girl! he thought as he focused on the amazing beast that was eyeing up the two sets of riders with its jet-black eyes.

The griffin was roughly the size of a horse. With the hindquarters of a lion and the forequarters of a gigantic eagle, the griffin embodied strength, pride and grace.

Elian was awestruck. The creature's fur glowed bright gold against the white snow, while its feathers gleamed as if polished in shades of brown, blue and deepest black. Razor-sharp talons and a wickedly curved beak gave fair warning that the griffin could be vicious. Ra had said that a griffin was one of the few creatures whose weapons were potent enough to harm a dragon. Despite being small in comparison to the enormous dragons, Elian could well believe that this fierce and beautiful creature would make a formidable fighter.

A dragon was in all likelihood more dangerous

than a griffin, yet Elian had quickly become comfortable in the presence of dragons. Ra had an aloof, imperious manner at times, but there was always a feeling of warmth underlining it. This deadly creature, however, had a cold air of superiority, and its proximity set Elian's heart racing. Its tufted tail swished from side to side as it swivelled its head around to regard each rider in turn.

'I am Karrok, speaker for my people,' it announced, rolling the 'r's and accenting the hard sounds. 'You're here to challenge for the second orb. We've been expecting you. Who seeks for us to release the dark orb so it may be taken to the Oracle?'

'I do, Karrok. I'm Pell, rider of Whispering Shadow.'

Elian was impressed that Pell could keep his voice so unflustered. Karrok's eyes were unnerving. Elian felt sure that if he were asked to speak now, he would not be able to hide his nervousness under that penetrating gaze.

'Which is as it should be,' the griffin said again, his eyes darting to look at Shadow over Pell's shoulder. 'Who seeks for us to release the dark orb so you may destroy it?'

Elian had expected Segun to step forwards, but he was surprised when the leader of the night dragon enclave called his men into a huddle and began whispering to them. After a moment they split again and one of the leader's lieutenants took a half-step forwards and spoke.

'I seek to destroy the orb, Karrok,' he announced. 'My name is Dirk, rider of Knifetail.'

*'Ware ye the knife . . . 'ware ye the knife.* Alarm bells rang in Elian's ears as the words of the Oracle's rhyme sprang into his mind. The man looked immensely strong. He had a huge chest and arms, with muscles enough to crush a bear.

'Accepted,' the griffin said simply. 'Pell, do you know the history of this challenge?'

'No,' he replied. 'The Oracle's rhyme led us here to seek your counsel in finding the orb.'

'And you, Dirk – do you know the history of this challenge?'

'No,' the big man said, glancing at his leader for reassurance. Segun did not meet his eyes. He looked back at the griffin. 'I do this at my leader's bidding.'

'All is as it should be,' the griffin cried. 'The challenge comprises three parts. We griffins will release the orb to the first rider to win two of three. Do you understand?'

Pell stared past the griffin and locked eyes with his adversary. 'Yes,' they said together.

267

'Challengers,' Karrok said, turning his head to face Pell. 'It was here that both previous quests failed. Griffins remain impartial in dragon affairs. The life or death of the Oracle is of no concern to us. We judge your contest and enforce fair play to honour an ancient agreement made with the dragonriders who brought us here. Come. Both challengers mount your dragons and follow me. We shall prepare the first test.'

'And what of the rest of us?' Segun asked.

'Those who want to destroy the orb, fly along the left side of the valley,' Karrok ordered. 'Those who want to take it to the Oracle, fly along the right. Stray from my instructions at your peril. We do not wish to harm you or your dragons, but we will be swift to punish any who do not comply. Look for the metal stand. Land there and observe the challenges. Stay on your respective sides. Griffins will be watching.'

Karrok's threat seemed ludicrous. How could a few griffins hope to enforce Karrok's orders to *ten* dragons? Elian chanced a look up at the cliff on the far side of the canyon. He blinked in surprise and rubbed at his eyes, wondering if they were playing tricks on him. Then he looked up at the near side and saw the same again. The valley was suddenly full of griffins – hundreds of them. Some were sitting, lined up on ledges like rows of huge painted gargoyles, and some were prowling along the top of the first tier of the great mountainsides. Others still were airborne, flying in long lines high up along the sides of the valleys.

'*It looks like those few griffins that first came here have been busy!*' he observed to Aurora. '*Where did all these come from?*'

'*I do not know, Elian,*' she replied, similarly surprised. '*But it would be unwise to anger them. A dragon might overcome one or two griffins, but a host like this . . .*'

Aurora did not need to complete the thought. Elian turned to Pell and put a hand on the older boy's shoulder. It was all down to him now. 'Good luck,' Elian said simply, glancing over his shoulder at the senior night dragonriders who were walking back to their dragons. From the look of Pell's adversary, he was going to need it.

Pell felt both nervous and excited at the same time. Following the night dragons into this valley had been a dangerous gamble. Despite the odds, he had won a chance to get the orb without a fight. All he had to do was beat Segun's man at whatever challenges Karrok set. Knifetail looked a formidable dragon, but she would not intimidate Shadow. Nor would Dirk intimidate him.

'*This is our chance to show Segun,*' he said silently to Shadow as he turned towards her. '*If we're going to be outlaws, then let's make that dungball wish he'd never crossed us.*'

'*Sounds good to me,*' Shadow replied, her voice soft and deadly.

Pell was a little startled at Elian's touch on his shoulder. The boy wished him 'Good luck', a message he acknowledged with a nod. He half expected the two girls to repeat the message, but one look at them was enough to dispel that thought. Nolita was too distracted to say anything, locked as usual in her own little world of fear. Kira, on the other hand, was more interested in giving him unwanted advice.

'Remember the rhyme,' Kira told him in a low voice. 'No doubt the words will start to make sense any time now. There was advice in your verse. Stay pure. Listen. Accept justice. Don't be tempted to do anything outside of the rules in order to win, Pell.'

'Thanks for that, Kira,' he replied, unable to totally mask the sarcasm in his reply. 'Wise words, I'm sure.'

'Did you hear what the griffin just said?' she asked, her anger barely restrained.

'I expect so,' he replied. 'Which part in particular?'

'The last two quests failed here,' Kira said bluntly. 'Not a great record for the night dragonriders, I'd say. And if they were as pig-headed and arrogant as you are, I'm not surprised they failed.'

With that, Kira turned on her heel and stomped across to Fang's side. Pell watched her go out of the corner of his eye. He did not want Elian and Nolita to see that she had got to him with her comments, so he did his best to keep his features composed and his apparent focus on Shadow. Inside, however, he knew there was something in what she had said. The Oracle would die if he failed. The words in the rhyme had been carefully chosen to give him the best chance of success. If Kira were not such an annoyance, he would have thanked her.

He sprang up Shadow's foreleg and swung into the saddle. Placing his feet into the stirrups, he let Shadow know he was ready to go. She sprang forwards at once, launching into the air to follow Karrok. Dirk on Knifetail quickly settled into formation alongside them.

The griffin flew steadily along the centre of the valley and Pell soon noticed the metal stand that

Karrok had mentioned. It looked very much like the plinth that Nolita had described when she found the first orb, though there was no sign of an orb here.

Karrok continued flying along the valley past the plinth and some distance further before swooping down to land on a large, snow-covered rock. The two night dragons followed him down, landing on a flat area just short of Karrok's vantage point.

The griffin turned to face the two dragons.

'You must attempt three tasks,' he cried, his harsh voice echoing slightly from the huge walls of rock on either side. 'The first task will test speed, coordination, judgement and bravery. You are to fly up the valley, adjusting your height until you are level with two griffins who will be hovering side by side, each holding a lance in their talons. They will wait until you pass a marker, then drop their lances. Your task is to each catch a lance before it hits the ground. If either dragon is below the height of the griffins when the lances are dropped, that dragon and rider will automatically lose the task.'

Pell's heart sank as he remembered Shadow's words that fateful day when he had fallen from her back. *'I've never been very good at catching.'* Shadow had caught him, but she had struggled. Catching a lance dropped from a much lower altitude was infinitely more difficult. The lance was likely to spin and tumble, making a catch difficult to judge and offering the potential to injure, or even kill, the catcher. Alternatively, it might spear downwards, streamlined and fast and impossible to catch up with. The chances of Shadow being able to catch a falling lance seemed very small.

'*How are you feeling today, Shadow?*' he asked, trying to sound upbeat. '*Ready to play catch?*'

'*I can think of things I'd rather do,*' she admitted. '*But I'll do my best.*'

'*Your best will be fine. No one can ask more than that. Not even the Oracle.*'

## Chapter Twenty-Two
# Battling it Out

Once they were airborne and climbing, Pell's nerves began to settle a little. Flying on Shadow's back with the wind in his hair and the familiar rhythm of her wingbeats was comforting. It made him feel complete. Dirk and Knifetail were climbing alongside them as the two pairs positioned themselves for the first task. Pell looked across at Dirk. The older rider looked confident and composed. Was that bravado?

'*Conserve your energy, Shadow,*' Pell told her, as he sensed her desire to show Knifetail who was the stronger dragon by climbing so fast that she couldn't keep up. '*We don't know what the other two tasks are yet. Let's not compete unnecessarily.*'

'*You are right, Pell. I was acting like a hatchling. Sorry.*' A moment later she spoke again. '*I see the two*

274

*griffins now. They are higher than I expected. That's good.'*

Pell scanned the sky. A breeze, nonexistent at ground level, chose that moment to gust and swirl, causing Shadow to dip and bump. The turbulence was only light, but it was uncomfortable and it added an unwanted level of difficulty to the search. It took a little while for his eyes to pick up the two tiny figures hovering high above the valley.

'Yes, I see them,' he confirmed. *'You're right, Shadow. They're being far more generous than I imagined. At least we'll have a fighting chance of making a catch before the lance hits the ground.'*

They circled round and round, climbing ever higher, until they approached the height of the griffins. By now the turbulence was more pronounced and the two dragons widened their formation to avoid an inadvertent clash of wings as they bounced around in the invisible maze of up- and down-drafts.

Without warning, Knifetail tightened her turn inside Shadow and began to make a run down the valley towards the griffins. Pell cursed aloud.

*'After them,'* he urged, but his thought was redundant, as Shadow had reacted at precisely that instant.

Dirk's dragon was fast, but Shadow was just a

shade faster. As she powered along at a level speed greater than Pell had ever experienced before, the rough air made it impossible to do any more than hang on as tightly as he could. Over the previous two years, Pell's stomach had become hardened to the lurching, bumping ride sometimes experienced on dragonback. However, the combination of nerves, excitement, and the sheer intensity of the turbulence at this moment brought the acid taste of sick up into the back of his mouth.

The wind and the bouncing blurred his vision. They were almost alongside Knifetail, when Shadow suddenly folded her wings and dipped headfirst into a screaming dive for the valley floor.

The lance! Pell was so focused on catching up with the other team, he had forgotten to look ahead at the griffins. Shadow was absolutely howling through the air now and Pell was leaning almost flat against her back. He was forced to squint so much against the blasting wind that his vision was limited to a fine line, obscured partially by his eyelashes. It was madness. Shadow bounced and bucked as she accelerated faster and faster, but Pell was oblivious to everything other than his search for the falling lance.

The grey rock of the valley walls was a blur and the bright white of the snow-covered valley basin seemed to swell as they hurtled earthwards. The pressure built painfully in his ears and he swallowed hard several times in quick succession to relieve the discomfort. All the time he was doing his best to see the lance. If it had not been for the snow, Pell doubted he would ever have spotted it, but suddenly there it was, spinning just below them. The brown of the wooden weapon stood out against the background of white as it spun. It looked long but slender.

'*Dive under it!*' The idea rocked Pell as he recognised their best chance of success. '*Don't try to catch it. Dive under it. I'll do the catching.*'

Shadow did not answer, but he felt her adjust her dive to an even steeper angle. He sensed her trust in him through the bond. He could only hope the trust was justified. There would be time for one attempt only. The grey rock-face of the walls was diminishing fast as they ran out of altitude.

With what seemed like painful slowness, Shadow caught up with the lance, diving past and underneath it. Pell picked his moment. He would have preferred to catch it with his right hand, but the lance was having none of it. He watched as the long wooden weapon spun, moving above him and to his left.

'*Now, Pell! It has to be now!*' Shadow urged. The sense of ground-rush was growing fast.

Gripping the pommel of the saddle in his right hand, Pell forced his body upright and reached out with his left hand. The force of the wind pushing against his chest was immense. The muscles in his right arm bulged and trembled as he fought with all his might against the force trying to tear him from Shadow's back. He gritted his teeth and let out a snarl of defiance at the wind as he stretched out further and further.

'*Up a bit,*' he growled aloud.

'*No time.*'

Shadow snapped her wings outwards and the great leathery expanses smacked against the airflow with immediate and dramatic effect. The dragon's effort to deflect their plummeting descent caused an abrupt difference in relative velocity between Pell and the lance. It suddenly whipped downwards like a giant quarterstaff, smacking into the V between his thumb and fingers with such force that for a moment he thought his thumb must have broken. His fingers instinctively closed around the shaft of the lance, but keeping a grip on it was difficult. Aside from the intense spike of pain from his thumb, the apparent weight of Pell's body and the lance suddenly multiplied by several factors as the force generated by Shadow's rapid turn crushed him against her back.

'AAAAARRRRRGGGGGGHHHHHH!'

The cry was involuntary. It squeezed out through tightly-gritted teeth, as he clenched his stomach muscles as hard as he could. Everything turned grey as the force peaked. In a last-ditch effort to retain consciousness, Pell tightened every other muscle in his body and focused every last drop of his energy into not letting go of the lance. Then it was over. The force reduced and the weight of the lance lightened. They were in level flight, skimming at high speed along the base of the valley.

'*Gods alive, Shadow!*' Pell exclaimed aloud as realisation dawned at just how low they were. '*You cut that fine!*'

'We *cut that fine, you mean,*' Shadow replied, her tone carrying a hint of reproof. '*Are you all right? I felt your pain as you caught the lance.*'

Pell had transferred the lance to his right hand to avoid inadvertently dropping it, but it was nearly impossible to grip the pommel with his left hand. His left thumb was throbbing and, although he could just about move it, he could not put any pressure on it without experiencing extreme pain.

'*I caught the lance awkwardly and hurt my thumb, but it's not too bad,*' he replied. As the words passed his lips he wondered if they were as much for his own benefit as they were for his dragon. '*Where are Dirk and Knifetail?*' he asked, looking around. He could not see them anywhere.

'*Behind and above us.*'

Pell looked over his shoulder. Knifetail was a good hundred spans above them and Pell could see she was gripping a lance in her talons.

'Damn!' he muttered. 'I wonder what happens now.'

Shadow used the last of her momentum from the long dive to ease up into a tight climbing turn to the right. They rolled out of the turn and flew back to where they knew Karrok was waiting. A couple of minutes later, they landed back at the far end of the canyon. Knifetail and Dirk landed next to them. Pell dismounted and placed the lance on the snow in front of Shadow.

Karrok regarded both dragons and riders impassively.

'Yours was a brave catch, Pell,' he said, his harsh voice carrying a note of respect. 'But Knifetail was first to catch a lance. Therefore Dirk and Knifetail win the first challenge.'

Pell's instinct was to protest immediately. When he had described the challenge, Karrok had said nothing about the fastest partnership to catch their lance. He opened his mouth, hot anger flaring and arguments boiling up inside him.

'*Yield unto justice.*' Shadow's unexpected quote from the Oracle's verse doused the flames of his anger so fast it left an icy aftershock in the pit of his stomach. Was this justice? He was not convinced. But despite his instant misgivings he clamped his mouth shut. He respected Shadow's judgement. '*Stay focused,*' she continued. '*There are two more tasks. We just have to win them both.*'

'*No pressure then,*' Pell growled silently. He glanced across at Dirk. The big man had a smirk on his face that fuelled the fire of Pell's anger. His thoughts raced through a hundred nasty things he would like to do to wipe the expression from his opponent's face, but Karrok chose that moment to begin briefing for the second challenge.

'The second task will test the coordination and daring of both dragons and riders,' Karrok began. 'Riders will take up the lances. You must now use them to collect five rings. Soon, if you look along the valley, you will see two lines of my brothers, one on either side, hovering at varying heights. The rings will be below them, suspended by lengths of string from their talons. Your friends are securing the rings as I speak.'

Pell was horrified. His hand to eye coordination

was good, but the lance was at least four spans long. Controlling the tip would be incredibly difficult whilst flying. Holding it in his right hand was no problem. His biggest difficulty would be staying on Shadow's back, as he had no gripping power with his left hand at all.

'You will start from here on my call,' Karrok continued. 'Once you have the rings, return them to me here. It will be a few more minutes before my brothers are in place. I suggest you rest until then.'

Pell inspected his left thumb. He had been unconsciously cradling it in his right hand ever since he had put the lance down. It did not look pretty. A dark purple bruise was blossoming all around its base and the lower half of it was swelling noticeably. He prodded the bruise gently with his finger and immediately regretted it. A spike of pain shot up his arm that set his eyes watering.

*'I never thought I'd say this, but having Firestorm here would be useful right now,'* he admitted to Shadow. *'It's no use. I'm not going to be able to stay in the saddle and use a lance if I've got to rely on my left hand for support.'*

*'Do you wish to yield?'* Shadow asked.

Pell knew from her voice that she would be devastated by that outcome, but yielding had never been in his nature. *'No! Of course not!'* he replied immediately. '*Lower your foreleg again, please. I need to climb back up. I've got some rope in my saddlebag. I'm going to tie my left hand to the saddle grip.*'

Pell grabbed the lance and made his way over to Shadow's side. He propped the lance upright in the crook of her foreleg and then climbed up into the saddle. It was awkward, but he managed it without too much trouble. The saddlebag was easy enough to open with one hand and after a moment or two of rummaging around he found what he was looking for.

The piece of rope was too long, so he wedged a short length under his knee, twisted the desired cut point between the fingers of his left hand and sawed through it with his belt knife. He inadvertently dropped the longer length. It slid to the ground, but he knew it was no loss. He had what he needed. Carefully sheathing his knife, Pell then tried to secure his left hand to the saddle grip at the pommel. It was hideously difficult and immensely frustrating. Time and again he twisted the rope into different knots, but no matter how hard he tried, he could not get them tight enough.

In the distance he saw the griffins begin to rise into the air in a stream. He was running out of time. It was a compromise, but rather than try to tie the knots tightly, he decided to use a couple of simple self-tightening slipknots instead. A double hitch onto the pommel grip, followed by the same around his wrist was completed just in time.

'Riders, take up your lances.'

Karrok's order made Pell jump. He leaned across and grabbed the shaft of his upright lance. With a shuffling sequence of mini throws and catches, he worked his right hand along the shaft until he had hold of the weapon in the correct place behind the hand-guard. It towered above him like a flagpole. He knew he couldn't fly with it like this, so he carefully lowered it at an angle across Shadow's back until the shaft was resting between two of her ridges. The point was about a span to the left of her head.

'*Don't turn your head to the left, Shadow,*' he warned. '*I don't want to take your eye out with this thing.*'

'*It is a little distracting there, Pell,*' she admitted. '*If you could raise the tip a bit once we're airborne, I'd appreciate it.*'

'*I'll do my best.*'

'Pell and Shadow, collect the rings from my brothers on the left of the valley,' Karrok ordered. 'Dirk and Knifetail, yours are on the right. Make ready.'

Shadow turned around to her right until she was

facing down the valley. Alongside her, Knifetail was doing the same.

'GO!'

Shadow accelerated forwards so fast that Pell rocked back in the saddle. The whiplash effect yanked the slipknot at his left wrist, tightening it painfully as he felt the lashing pass its first test. With his balance quickly restored, Pell leaned forwards and angled the tip of the lance upwards slightly as Shadow powered up into the air.

'*Aim to fly slightly below and to the right of the rings as we approach them,*' Pell told her, looking ahead along the line of the valley. The first of the griffins was clearly visible ahead. He could see the ring below the griffin. It seemed stable enough with its open mouth towards him. As they got closer he could see that it was bouncing up and down with each wingbeat of the griffin, so timing was crucial.

Pell raised the tip of the lance still further. It was good that he was concentrating to the left of Shadow. If he had been able to see Dirk and Knifetail out of the corner of his eye, the temptation to watch them would have been strong. The ring was approaching fast.

'*Smooth it out as we approach,*' Pell ordered. Shadow complied, using her momentum to soar the final couple of dragon-lengths without beating her wings in order to give Pell a stable platform from which to spear the ring. In those final few moments Pell concentrated furiously on the rhythm of the ring's rise and fall. He could see instantly why the ring was so stable. There was not one string holding the ring, but two: one from each of the griffin's taloned feet.

His judgement was perfect, dipping the tip of the lance into the very centre of the hoop. There was a very slight tug on the lance as the strings broke and then Shadow was turning right and descending towards the next griffin, which was considerably lower than the first. Pell shot a swift glance at Knifetail and Dirk. They were a fraction behind, but Dirk too had secured his first ring. There was no time to worry about them further. The next ring was approaching.

The angle of approach this time was not so easy. They were descending and Shadow had taken a very slight turn to the left to prepare their exit angle for the next target. Pell fixed his focus on the ring, but he could not work out the rhythm of its rise and fall. Before he knew it, he had hit the bottom of the ring with the tip of the lance. One of the strings snapped instantly and the ring flashed past his head, spinning round and round on the one remaining cord.

'Damn!' he swore aloud.

'*Don't worry,*' Shadow told him calmly. '*We'll get it on the way back. Keep your focus.*'

As they approached the third ring, Pell realised things were not getting any easier. The rings were becoming progressively smaller. When he neatly snagged the third onto his lance he could see the difference in size immediately.

The fourth ring was approaching fast. It was untidy, but with a dramatic lunge at the last instant, he somehow managed to sneak the point into the inside right edge. The ring lodged on the tip of the lance, but didn't slide safely to the hilt. The weight of the lance was increasing all the time, but by heaving the tip upwards and giving it a quick shake, Pell managed to dislodge the ring and slide it to safety.

Distracted by the need to secure the fourth ring, Pell did not anticipate Shadow's turn. As she began banking to the right to gain position for her run at the final ring, Pell was taken by surprise. He instinctively tried to grab the pommel with his left hand and cried out from the intense shock of pain that shot up his arm from his thumb. His grip failed and there was a new shock of pain as the cord bit deep into his wrist with the sudden load. Hauling his body back into balance, Pell looked up for the final ring. The ring looked tiny. It took the briefest pause for him to realise this was because it *was* tiny. Then it slotted onto the tip of his lance. He was not quite sure how he did it. Luck? Instinct? He didn't know. He had it and that was all that mattered.

'*Well done, Pell! Dirk missed his last one,*' Shadow told him, clearly elated that Pell had managed to secure the final ring. '*Hang on. I'll take us back for the one we missed.*'

'*Do we need it?*' Pell asked as Shadow began a hard turn to the right. '*If Dirk missed one as well, that makes four each. If the last test was anything to go by, then the first one back now will win.*'

'*Karrok was quite specific,*' Shadow insisted. '*He said, "Once you have the rings . . ." which means we must get them all.*'

'*All right, then. Let's go.*'

They rolled out of the turn. Pell's arm was aching with the effort of holding the lance. It had not seemed heavy to begin with, but now it felt as if it were made of lead. His right wrist and bicep were burning with the effort of keeping the tip up high enough to prevent the rings from sliding down and off the end.

He looked ahead. There was only one griffin in front of them. The four from whom he had successfully taken rings had flown out of the way. As soon as he saw the ring he knew that he was in trouble. Not only was it bobbing up and down and swinging back and forth from the impact of his lance, now that it was hanging by a single cord, it was also spinning. It was one of the larger rings, but Pell knew it could prove the hardest to collect.

Shadow began to slow down, positioning herself for the run.

'*Don't slow down,*' Pell urged. '*Go for it. I'll hit it, or I won't, but we still need to beat Dirk back to Karrok.*'

Shadow did not need to be told twice. Her head stretched forwards and her wings accelerated them towards the ring with every stroke. The griffin began to loom and the ring swung and spun like a child's yo-yo on its string. Pell raised the tip of his lance a touch further, his eyes unblinking as they approached. The ring swung towards them and Pell dipped the lance at it even as it twisted. For the slightest instant he thought he had missed, but the familiar tug on the lance as the final cord snapped sent a shock of elation through him.

'*Got it! Go, go, go!*' he urged.

Already flying fast, Shadow accelerated still further as they tore down the valley to where Karrok was waiting. Shadow swooped down and backwinged to a most dramatic landing just a handful of paces short of the griffin. Pell tilted his lance, allowing the five rings to spill along its length and fall to ground by Karrok's talons. The griffin looked down at the small pile of rings.

A whoosh of air and a whumpf announced Knifetail's less elegant arrival a few moments later. The griffin looked up.

'Well done,' Karrok acknowledged. 'Both teams showed considerable skill, but Pell and Shadow claim victory in the second task.'

# Chapter Twenty-Three
# The Knife

As Shadow landed next to Aurora, Pell was awash with emotion. He could almost taste relief at the back of his tongue. He and Shadow had not disgraced themselves in the first two challenges, so he could hold his head high in front of the others. At the same time his muscles were taut with nervous tension as he worried about the nature of the final task. He and Dirk had been sent with their dragons back to their respective parties to rest. Apparently, the griffins had to make preparations for the final test.

'That was amazing!' Elian enthused, running to Shadow's side as Pell dismounted. 'You and Shadow can really fly! Those challenges looked well dangerous from down here. Especially that mad dive on the first task. How are you feeling?'

Elian's right hand was extended in greeting. Pell clasped it in his. A rush of warmth at Elian's genuine enthusiasm took him by surprise. He knew he made it difficult for others to get close. It was an inbuilt defence mechanism that he had developed over the years to avoid hurt and disappointment. His experience was that friendships always led to pain. It was his own fault. His personal ambition and drive inevitably turned people against him. From the beginning of this quest, he had deliberately held his companions at a cold distance, but Elian appeared determined to ignore the barriers.

'I've felt better,' Pell admitted.

Kira was not far behind Elian and, to Pell's surprise, he could see respect in her eyes. Nolita stood some distance away. Her eyes watched Shadow, full of terror. She would come no closer.

'That was some pretty fancy flying, Pell,' Kira said grudgingly. 'You did well to beat Dirk on that second task. Those lances are so long, they must be a nightmare to handle.'

'Thanks,' he said, not knowing what else to say.

'Do you know what the final challenge is?' she added.

He shook his head. 'We were just told it would take a short while for the griffins to set it up.'

Pell glanced across the base of the valley to where

the night dragonriders were huddled around Dirk. Segun was talking very earnestly with them and gesturing. One of the riders – not Dirk – broke away from the group and walked to his dragon.

'I wonder what that's all about?' Pell mused aloud.

'I don't know, but it looks as though Segun is up to something,' Kira observed, her eyes narrowing as she watched the rider mount.

'Whatever it is, he's unlikely to do anything to annoy the griffins, unless he's either very brave or very stupid,' Elian said confidently. 'There are hundreds of them up there. Who would have ever thought there would be this many?'

'I wouldn't put it past Segun to try to slip something past the griffins' attention,' Pell said thoughtfully. 'But you're right. Karrok doesn't strike me as a fool. Come. I need to ask a favour of Nolita.'

Pell strode away from Shadow's side towards their blond companion. Elian glanced across at Kira, whose eyes had widened with much the sort of surprise that he felt. Until now, Pell had shown nothing but contempt for Nolita. What favour could he possibly want from her? Whatever it was, it looked as though Pell was about to show a degree of humility they would not have believed possible.

Neither of them wanted to miss what he had to say, so they hurried after him, slipping and sliding across the snow-covered, rocky ground.

'Pell.' Nolita acknowledged his approach with a nod. 'I'm glad this challenge fell to you. I could never have done what you just did.'

Pell smiled at the admission. 'I have a feeling that the Oracle chose each of us specifically to face the particular challenges that awaited us,' he replied. 'You passed your challenge, Nolita. I've got work to do to match your achievement, and I think I'm going to need your help to succeed.'

'My help?' she squeaked. 'I can't do the sort of things you just did.'

'No, and I wouldn't ask you to,' he replied. 'But that's not what I mean. I injured my left hand when I caught the lance during the first task. The pain nearly caused me to lose the second. Could you ask Firestorm if he will heal it for me, please? It would help a lot if I faced the final challenge without this distracting me.'

Pell held his left hand out. Nolita winced as she took in the deep, purple-black bruising and the obvious swelling around the base of his thumb.

'Of course,' she said quickly. 'I'm sure Firestorm will help. Perhaps this is what the Oracle meant by working together.'

Pell did not care whether it was what the Oracle meant or not. He wanted to win. If that meant begging aid from Nolita, then he would do it. All that mattered now was beating Segun's man. If his companions felt he was working with them for the benefit of the Oracle, then that was fine. The truth was, he wanted to poke Segun in the eye for imprisoning him at the enclave. By winning through this series of challenges, he knew he would set Segun's plans back and undermine his credibility as a leader. What better outcome could there be?

One of the night dragons launched into the air. The whooshing wingbeats sounded loud in the silence of the cold valley, but then gradually faded into the distance, as dragon and rider made for the tunnel that led out of the canyon. Pell kept his focus on Nolita.

'Firestorm tells me he heard our conversation through my mind and he is happy to heal your hand,' she said, her eyes going distant for an instant as she communicated with her dragon. 'Go to him and he'll do it straight away.'

'Thank you,' he said simply.

Pell turned to where the day dragon was crouched. His blue scales looked particularly bright against the white background of the snow. Although he was nowhere near as physically impressive as

Shadow, Pell found himself admiring Firestorm's appearance.

There was something handsome and noble in Firestorm's bearing that he had never noticed before. But he wasn't really interested in any dragon other than Shadow. He simply wanted Firestorm's help.

He walked forwards until he was standing directly in front of Firestorm. The blue dragon eyed him impassively and, for the slightest moment, Pell felt as if Firestorm could see what he was thinking. He clenched his teeth together tightly and fought down the sudden urge to turn and run. Firestorm drew in a deep, slow breath and Pell held out his left hand towards the dragon's mouth. Then it happened.

Pell had not been conscious the last time Firestorm had healed him, so he had no idea what to expect. In his mind he had imagined the healing flame would be somehow very precise, targeting the area of the wound. The reality was something of a shock. His first instinct was to close his eyes as the great blue nimbus of flame engulfed him, but as soon as he realised that the fire held no apparent heat, he cracked his eyelids open again to watch. The blue flames swirled and danced, causing his skin to prickle and his hair to float about his head like a ball of fine yellow seaweed, gently caressed by unseen currents.

The prickling was most intense around the wound on his left hand, but it did not hurt. Indeed, he could feel the fire penetrating through the skin of his thumb and working its healing miracle deeper and deeper into the flesh. He lifted the hand in front of his face and marvelled at the changes he could see. The swelling was reducing and the darkness of the bruising was dispersing. Once again he felt invigorated, much as he had done when he had awoken after his previous healing. As Firestorm finally ran out of breath and the blue fire died away, Pell was ecstatic.

He bowed to the dragon with what he hoped was suitable respect, turned, and repeated the gesture to Nolita. She blushed a deep crimson, and Pell could see instantly that the effort had not been wasted. Elian and Kira looked as if they were in shock. He had them off balance. Good. They had proved they could be resourceful. If he could manipulate them and use their skills to his advantage, they could prove to be a real thorn in Segun's side.

As he and Shadow were outlawed, it would not hurt to have allies with such an unusual mix of abilities in future encounters with the night dragon enclave. Kira would be the trickiest to control. Even now he could see the cynicism in her expression. He would have to keep her off balance and play along nicely with the quest for a while as if he really cared. If he worked at it, he felt sure he could win her round.

'Do you think we have time for food?' he asked. 'I'm suddenly feeling really hungry.'

'I think we could all probably use a bite,' Elian replied. 'We could eat some of the cold food.'

The four scattered to their respective dragons and rummaged through their saddlebags. Even as Pell was digging through his bag, he noticed the night dragon returning along the valley.

'*The griffins prevented her from leaving,*' Shadow told him. '*I sense that Widewing is not pleased. Whatever Segun was planning is unlikely to happen now.*'

'*Good,*' Pell responded, his mood lightening even further. '*Anything that goes wrong for Segun is fine by me.*'

He rejoined the others and they brushed snow from some rocks so they could sit down without getting wet. The rocks made cold seats, but the four riders made themselves as comfortable as possible and proceeded to eat their food.

They watched in silence as the night dragon-riders met their returning companion. Pell expected

Segun to be furious, but after a quick conference he looked remarkably composed and satisfied.

'What was that all about?' Kira mused aloud.

'Segun looks smug,' Elian said. 'You'd better watch yourself on the last challenge, Pell. I don't like the look of that.'

What the rider could have achieved by flying to the end of the valley and back, Pell could not begin to imagine. One thing was certain – Elian was right. It did not bode well.

It was some time before they finally spotted Karrok flying towards them along the base of the valley. The griffin landed by the metal plinth.

'Challengers, mount your dragons,' he called out in a loud voice. 'Your final challenge will be a test of endurance and speed. You will race out of this valley and follow a series of markers that have been laid out to lead you along a route through the mountain valleys. The first team to return to the plinth having completed the course will claim release of the orb. Griffins have laid markers on the ground at turning points along the route. They will observe the turning points to ensure both dragons complete the whole course. You will see the first marker as you exit the valley.'

Pell was delighted. He felt sure that Shadow was stronger and faster than Knifetail. Unlike the previous challenges, this was one he felt sure they could win. He ran to Shadow and leaped up her side and into the saddle. He could see Dirk settling on Knifetail's back. It had all come down to a simple race. If the Oracle had told him this at the start, he would likely have laughed. It seemed a ridiculous way to determine the future of dragon-kind.

'Ready . . . GO!'

There was no further time for thought. Shadow powered forwards with Knifetail matching her, stride for stride, wingbeat for wingbeat. They climbed into the air, but neither dragon climbed more than a few spans. Instead, all power was converted into forward motion as they accelerated faster and faster in a sprint for position at the end of the valley. Each dragon was determined to reach the exit tunnel first. Whoever held the lead there looked set to have the edge for the rest of the route.

The valley began to narrow. Still both dragons held position. Pell glanced across at Knifetail. The dragon seemed to be using her tail as an extra form of propulsion, lashing it from side to side. The motion made her look ungainly in comparison to Shadow, but Pell could not deny that she was keeping pace with them. Pell noticed something else about the lashing tail. On either side of its final span or so, there was a shallow plate-like protrusion of bone that looked flat and sharp. The dragon was not called Knifetail without reason. Pell instantly recognised the lethal nature of such a weapon. If he and Shadow were to fall behind Knifetail, passing her could prove extremely hazardous – and not just for him. The natural dragonbone blade on her tail could potentially slice through Shadow's armour as well.

'*Come on, Shadow!*' he urged, leaning forwards to the right of the ridge in front of him and flattening himself against her back in the most streamlined fashion he could. '*You can do it.*'

They were running out of room. The valley was narrowing fast as they entered the final bend and the two dragons were all but wingtip to wingtip as they raced around the corner towards the tunnel. The throat of the valley forced the dragons closer and closer together. Pell was watching for trouble, half expecting Knifetail to pull some nasty trick in order to take the lead into the tunnel. To his surprise, the dragon dropped back, allowing Shadow to lead the way out of the valley.

Shadow dipped her wing and turned hard into the exit tunnel. Pell squeezed his muscles against the huge force that crushed him against Shadow's back as they whipped around the corner on a wingtip. Being flat to her back, the effects of the pressing force were reduced, but he was glad to be able to grip securely with both hands, or he might have slid out of the saddle. They rolled out of the turn inside the tunnel and powered towards the bright opening ahead.

'*Turning hard right*,' Shadow warned.

Suddenly they were in the open. Pell barely had time to register the flash of blue on the ground before Shadow was into the turn and he was being crushed against her back again. They rolled out and Shadow resumed beating her wings with the urgent tempo she had established in the valley.

'*How long can you keep up this pace?*' Pell asked as he glanced over his shoulder at Knifetail and Dirk who had dropped behind by a few dragon-lengths. '*We don't know how long this route is going to be.*'

'*It doesn't matter how long the route is, Pell,*' she replied. '*Knifetail will burn out before I do. I am strong. You know this. We will win this race.*'

She was right. In terms of pace, he would bet on Shadow against any other dragon, with the possible exception of Widewing. Segun's dragon was even bigger than Shadow. Although he would have liked to defeat the night dragon leader directly, rather than one of his lieutenants, Pell was a lot more confident of success than he would have been racing against the formidable Widewing.

Pell could see another blue marker on the ground ahead. The colour stood out clearly against the white of the snow. The valley forked in front of them and the blue line of cloth indicated a right turn. He looked around for the watching griffin and soon located it. The creature was perched on a rock, high up on the dividing wall between the two valleys.

A glance over his shoulder and Pell could see that Knifetail was slowly falling further behind. They took the valley to the right; the great mountains on either side towering up into the sky like monstrous pointed teeth. A chill wind began to gust and swirl. High in the sky above, white wispy horsetails of cirrus gave warning that the long spell of good weather was finally coming to an end. It would be some hours yet before Pell needed to worry about lower cloud bringing trouble. Even so, it was not a good sign. He would rather not be in the mountains come nightfall, as conditions could become dangerous very quickly.

The valley curved gently to the right. Ahead was another marker – black this time – indicating a sharp turn to the right. At first Pell could not see the opening, but then the narrow crack in the cliff-face became apparent.

'*Gods alive!*' he breathed aloud. '*Can we fit through there?*'

'*I think so,*' Shadow replied. '*But it's going to be tight.*'

She took a slightly wider line into the cut so they could see into the canyon before they entered. It looked treacherously narrow, barely wide enough for a dragon with Shadow's wingspan. It was slightly wider higher up, but if they climbed, they would inevitably lose speed. There were wickedly jagged rocks protruding from the walls on either side, poised to catch on a wingtip and there was no clear path through to the far side.

'*Hold on tight. This is going to get interesting.*'

Pell was so focused on the treacherous path ahead that it did not cross his mind to look for the watching griffin until it was too late. As they entered the canyon he flicked a quick look over his shoulder and was just in time to see Knifetail fly past the entrance without so much as twitching towards it. In that instant, he knew they had been fooled.

'*It's a trap, Shadow!*' he gasped. '*Dirk and Knifetail carried straight on. Somehow we've been set up.*'

He could feel Shadow's anger through the link

like a brewing storm, but she was concentrating so hard on not hitting the canyon walls that she could not release her feelings. They could not descend, for the crevasse beneath them continued to narrow to a fine wedge shape. Shadow was likely to break her wings if she tried. If they climbed, there was no room to turn until they reached the open sky many spans above.

Dipping and weaving through the perilous crack in the mountainside, Shadow fought to keep them in the air. A sudden, horrible revelation struck Pell as they wormed deeper into the canyon. *'Ware ye the knife*. This was the knife! The crack they had entered was so narrow it looked almost as if a knife blade had sliced a jagged path into the mountainside. A moment later the horror got worse. They were facing a dead-end. There was nowhere to go. One way or another they were going to crash into a rock-face and fall.

'*We're not done yet, Pell,*' Shadow said suddenly, her voice fierce with determination. '*I once saw a mad young dragon do a manoeuvre that might just save us. I've never tried this before, so let's hope I get it right. Hold on as tight as you can. We're going vertical.*'

'*Vertical?*' Pell exclaimed.

There was no time for Shadow to explain. The

next Pell knew, he was being crushed into the saddle. It felt as if they had entered a steeply banked turn, but instead of turning sideways, Shadow angled both wings at once into the airflow, tipping them upwards from level flight into a vertical climb.

Up, up, up they soared, losing energy all the way. No sooner were they climbing vertically than Shadow moved them a quarter turn to the right, so that her legs and back were climbing parallel to the walls of the canyon. The wind of their passage died away quickly to an eerie silence as they ran out of speed, and Pell felt his bottom gently detach from the saddle as all motive force ceased. Hanging onto the pommel grips for all he was worth, he found his legs were also losing their grip on Shadow's sides.

In the last moments of upward flight, Shadow eased towards the rock-face until her feet were running up the rock wall. She then stuck her tail out as far to the left as she could, using it like the rudder of a boat. Her upper body started to tilt to the left, and as it did so, she scrabbled at the cliff with her talons, helping her body around the turn until she was running vertically down again.

Pell began to fall sideways from Shadow's back. Only his grip on the pommel handles and his boots twisted firmly into the stirrups saved him. As she plummeted back downwards into the narrowing crack, Pell's panic grew. His only points of contact with Shadow were his hands and feet. She rolled gently to the right through another quarter turn, and he turned his body in sympathy, using his hands and feet as levers. Terrifying though this was, Pell was even more ill-prepared for the final part of Shadow's manoeuvre.

The instant she began to pitch out of the dive, Pell reconnected with the saddle – hard. The impact brought tears to his eyes as pain exploded in his groin from the crunching collision. Fortunately, he landed square into the saddle, or he would not have been able to hold on. The familiar force crushing him against Shadow's back increased the pain still further as she pitched them out of the dive, accelerating all the time. The wind tore through his hair as they hurtled back along the cut, whipping away his tears and blinding him with its force as he clung with a death-grip to the pommel handles.

Agony blinded Pell as Shadow weaved her way back out of the knife at a tremendous speed. They burst out into the open valley like a rock flung from a catapult.

'*Look!*' Shadow's voice roared in his mind. The single word rode on a wave of fury through the bond.

A black dragon was launching from the valley basin beneath them. It was carrying the marker in its talons.

## Chapter Twenty-Four
# The Second Orb

'Leave it, Shadow!' Pell groaned. 'It's not Knifetail. I don't know how Segun set this up, but there's no time for vengeance. We have to catch up with Knifetail and Dirk before they beat us to the orb.'

Shadow roared aloud this time, venting her anger with such passion that the black dragon below veered away instinctively. There were no griffins in sight – no witnesses to what had happened, aside from the perpetrators.

For a moment Pell thought Shadow might ignore him and dive on the fleeing night dragon, but she turned hard to the right to follow Knifetail and Dirk along the valley. Their opponents were already out of sight around the next bend, so catching them would not be easy. Fuelled by her anger at the lethal trap that had been laid, Shadow drove forwards at a pace Pell would never have believed possible. The ferocity with which she pounded the air with her wings was phenomenal and Pell knew they must be catching up with Dirk and Knifetail at a tremendous rate.

The valley ahead curved gently around to the right. At the far end was another marker – blue again. A griffin was watching over the turn point. They should have realised the last marker was a different colour, Pell thought. He cursed himself for the inattention that had nearly cost them their lives.

They cut the corner tight, flashing past the rock-face at the side of the valley and rolling out into the next to resume the frenetic, pounding rhythm. Knifetail was visible ahead now. She and Dirk had a good lead, but it was not insurmountable if Shadow kept up her current pace. Knifetail was flying with a comparatively sedate rhythm and Pell could see that she and her rider were not yet aware of Shadow.

'Shadow, can you use your silent flying ability at this speed?' Pell asked her.

'It won't be perfect, but I see what you are thinking,' she answered. 'They look like they're out for a pleasure flight. As we get closer, I'll slow a little to see if we can take them completely by surprise.'

The noise generated by Shadow's great wingbeats

suddenly dropped to a whisper and Pell's ears popped with the sudden change in the air around him. He had experienced Shadow's ability several times, but the transition always felt strange. The bubble of masked sound deadened the air, though his hair still streamed behind him as they raced along the snowy valleys.

Another blue marker was visible ahead. It was another right turn. They closed the distance to around twenty dragon-lengths as Knifetail dipped her wing and banked around the corner. Pell saw Dirk look over his shoulder. The big man started at the sight of them closing from behind.

'*Dirk's seen us!*' Pell yelled aloud. '*Forget stealth. We're back in a straight race again.*'

Pell's ears popped a second time as Shadow unmasked her sound signature and the wind-rush amplified back to full volume. He felt her straining through the bond. Fatigue burned through her body with a hungry, consuming fire. She was giving her all and Pell could feel the cost in every fibre of his body.

'*Come on, Shadow!*' he urged her again. '*You can do it. Not far to go now.*'

It was true. The valley they had entered was the one that concealed the entrance to the griffins' vale. They had flown full circle. Looking ahead,

Pell could just make out the marker outside the cunningly disguised tunnel.

From somewhere way beyond her normal reserves of strength, Pell felt Shadow draw on a deep source of energy that even she did not realise was there. Despite Knifetail's best efforts to accelerate away, every stroke of Shadow's wings closed the gap between the dragons. From directly behind the lashing tail of their adversary, Shadow eased to the right, edging into a position to overtake. Knifetail responded immediately, sliding across to block her. Shadow reversed to the left, but Knifetail was too quick. She was there, blocking the way and keeping them at bay with her lethal tail. The deadly swishing as it whipped back and forth warned of the power with which Knifetail was wielding her natural weapon.

Dipping and weaving, Shadow fought for position, but as they reached the markers for the tunnel, Knifetail was still successfully blocking their path. Pell could just make out the opening as they hurtled towards it. His heart leaped with instinctive fear as they entered. The thumping of the dragons' wingbeats echoed from the walls as they raced towards the tight turn into the secret vale. Their only chance now was to pass Knifetail in the final sprint for the plinth.

Both dragons took the corner at speed, rolling hard until they were turning on their wingtips to avoid crashing into the wall of rock at the far end of the tunnel. The force of the turn pressed Pell hard against Shadow's back, leaving him breathless and with swarms of dancing gold spots before his eyes as they rolled out.

Shadow began to weave from side to side in the narrow canyon, flying so close to the rock walls at times that Pell was convinced she would catch a wingtip. Then the valley widened ahead of them. Shadow feinted to the left and Knifetail began to respond. Even as she did so, Shadow reversed to the right and dived to convert every bit of energy she possessed into one last burst of speed.

Pell was at one with her through the bond. He instinctively leaned into the diving turn and focused ahead to the two parties waiting by the plinth. The explosion of pain in his shoulder took him completely by surprise. He screamed as the agony of the wound took his mind to the brink of unconsciousness and Shadow roared in unison. For that brief instant, darkness and oblivion loomed, but his cry of agony turned to one of rage as he realised what had happened. The pain was not his, but Shadow's. Knifetail's weapon had finally found its mark. In that moment of complete focus, he had

313

been so closely linked to her mind that he had mistaken the deep slicing wound Knifetail had dealt to Shadow's shoulder as his own.

Blood streamed down Shadow's side, but worse, Knifetail had gained an unbeatable position. Shadow did her best to recover, but it was no good and moments later Knifetail landed next to the plinth just a length or two ahead of them. Dirk punched the air in triumph and Pell's heart sank. He could not believe it. They had lost and the orb would now be claimed and destroyed by Segun. The Oracle would die, and its death would be his fault.

Claiming that Dirk and Knifetail had cheated would do no good. How could he prove it? The evidence was long gone.

He could see the looks on his companions' faces. They were devastated. The quest had failed. He had failed them. What could he say? He wanted to explain, but he felt so choked he could not find the words.

'*I'm sorry, Pell,*' Shadow said softly, her disappointment as profound as his own. '*I wasn't strong enough.*'

'*Don't be silly. You were magnificent,*' he replied. '*No rider could have asked more of his dragon. It's incredible that we're still alive, given the trap they set for*

314

us. We'd better ask Firestorm if he'll heal that wound of yours. It looks really nasty.'

'He can't.'

'Of course he can. You saw him heal me earlier.'

'Yes, but you're not a night dragon,' she said, her soft tones full of regret. 'A day dragon's healing power does not work on night dragons.'

'That's ridiculous! Why in blazes not?' he asked.

'Day and night dragons have always been diametrically opposed,' Shadow said sadly. 'Perhaps it is a part of our fundamental incompatibility.'

'Whatever that means!' Pell replied. 'Let's ask him and see, shall we?'

He dismounted, but he had hardly taken a handful of steps across the short distance to where Nolita and the others were standing, when Karrok spoke. The griffin's voice was powerful, demanding attention.

'Dirk and Knifetail, you have won the final challenge,' he began. 'Dirk, please join your companions. Knifetail, please remain where you are, for you have won the right to reveal the dark orb.'

Pell looked up at the sound of many sets of wings overhead. A pride of griffins were descending in a circle above them. He wondered what would happen now. A strange chill caused his flesh to rise into bumps. Whatever it was, the circling griffins were giving off a menacing aura that set him hurrying across to join his companions.

'What happened?' Elian asked. 'I thought you and Shadow would thrash Dirk and Knifetail in a race.'

'They cheated,' Pell replied. 'Somehow they got a message out to that group of riders we met a few days ago. They set us a nasty trap that we didn't see coming.'

'Why don't you say something, then?' Elian asked, his voice sounding desperate.

Kira stepped in immediately. '*Yield unto justice: truth will succeed*,' she quoted. 'Let's wait and see what happens before we say anything we might regret.'

Dirk had reached the other night dragonriders. The group were celebrating with him, shaking his hand and clapping him on the back – all except Segun. The leader of the night dragon enclave was standing quietly to one side of the group watching Knifetail and the spiralling cluster of griffins.

Without warning, the griffins all folded their wings and dived at Knifetail, their razor sharp talons extended to attack. The dragon stood no chance. Disappearing under a mass of tearing talons, she thrashed and slashed with her tail to no avail. She was tired after her long flight and even with the strength born from her fear and desperation, she could not shake off the ferocious griffins.

Dirk cried out as he realised what was happening, and it took all four of his fellow lieutenants to hold him from running headlong into the flurry of feathers, talons and beaks. Segun watched impassively.

Knifetail gave a scream of pain that tugged at Pell's sense of pity. The griffins, however, showed no mercy. Another scream, weaker this time, tailed off to silence. It was over. She was dead, but still the griffins ripped and tore at her with ferocious intent.

In a daze, Dirk turned to Segun and suddenly it was as if a light had been turned on in his mind. Pell could see the change in the man's features as his friends found themselves straining to hold him back again, this time from assaulting their leader.

'You knew!' he yelled, his face puce with anger. 'You knew all along and you didn't tell me! You killed my dragon! You!'

Segun turned to face Dirk, his face still emotionless.

'Yes, I knew,' he admitted. 'That was why I did not take up the challenge myself. The tale of the previous quests was written in the journals of past enclave leaders. It was not appropriate for me to sacrifice Widewing. The enclave needs me to lead them in the coming days. You, on the other hand, should be glad. Your dragon has been martyred for the sake of all dragonkind. Her name will go down in history as the dragon that died to free her kind from slavery, and yours will be right alongside it.'

Dirk gave an angry roar and, despite there being four strong men holding him, somehow managed to wrench free from their grasp. Pell and his companions gasped as the big man made to attack Segun, but their flash of hope was dashed as the taller man rammed a blade into Dirk's chest before he managed to land a single blow. Dirk stood for a moment, his face a mask of pain and shock.

'I'm sorry,' Segun said calmly. 'But you left me no choice.'

Dirk collapsed first to his knees, and then face down on the ground, his hands clutching the knife buried in his chest. The snow slowly turned red around his body.

There was a flurry of wings and the griffins began to disperse from Knifetail's carcass, blood-spattered yet clearly untouched by the brutal nature of what they had just done. One of the griffins emerged from the crowd walking, rather than flying. It held a large, dripping lump of raw flesh dangling from its beak. It took a moment for Pell to identify the nature of the grisly prize that the griffin carried forwards so delicately. It was Knifetail's heart.

He heard Nolita retch behind him, but he did not turn. The griffin was walking towards the plinth. What was it going to do? Karrok bowed his head to the griffin that carried the heart in its beak and the creature gently settled the great lump of bloody meat on the top of the metal stand. For a moment nothing happened. Pell wanted to turn away, but he could not take his eyes from the plinth. It was like some gruesome sacrificial rite that savages performed to appease their pagan idols. It was both horrifying and yet darkly fascinating.

The change was subtle – a shimmer of translucence crept over the heart like a sheet of clear water, emanating from the plinth. The heart began to change shape as the clear substance started to contract, drawing the heart first into a sphere and then shrinking it, crushing the flesh into an impossible ball of dark matter that no longer looked as if it had ever been a part of any living creature. A pulse of energy momentarily flashed outwards from the dark orb that had once been Knifetail's heart and then it was still; inert and lifeless, but giving off an aura that sent a chill down the spines of every human in the valley.

'Behold the dark orb, released from Knifetail,

dragon of the night,' Karrok announced. 'Who claims it?'

'I do,' said Segun, his voice cold.

'Very well. Come forward, human.'

Pell was not sure whether to rejoice, or cry out in objection. If he and Shadow had won the final challenge, the heart that now formed the dark orb would have been that of his dragon. He could not help but feel happy that they had failed, though he knew the Oracle would now die because of their failure. Shadow was all he had. If she had been sacrificed in Knifetail's place, he would not have needed Segun to plunge a knife in his chest – he would have done it himself. Yet to see Segun walking forwards to claim the orb was almost more than he could bear.

Another flurry of wings drew his gaze upwards. A griffin descended, clearly tired. It cried out in its own language, a harsh and mournful cry that contained meaning, though what it said Pell could not interpret. Karrok stiffened.

'Hold!' he cried, his dark eyes stopping Segun in his tracks. 'My brother tells me that your people interfered with the final challenge. They diverted Shadow and Pell into The Knife. What do you have to say to this?'

'That's clearly nonsense,' Segun said quickly. 'No

dragon who entered The Knife could ever hope to escape with its life. Yet we all saw Shadow and Knifetail land almost alongside one another. It was a close contest. Dirk and Knifetail won. I claim the orb.'

'That is not the picture my brother paints,' Karrok said, his voice ominously threatening. 'Griffins do not lie, human, yet your kind are renowned for twisting your words.

'Pell, can you tell me what happened?'

Pell did so, describing the marker and how Shadow had flown the remarkable manoeuvre to turn them around in the death trap they had been led into. Karrok nodded.

'Your words smell of truth,' he said. 'Justice shall prevail here. Pell, take the orb.'

Segun took a step forwards and opened his mouth to protest, but the griffin's head snapped around to face him. One look at Karrok's eyes was enough to make Segun think twice. He closed his mouth and took a step backwards.

'We will hold the night dragons here,' Karrok told Pell. 'Take the orb and go. You are already aware that other night dragons lurk somewhere nearby. We cannot help you against those. You must find a way past them.'

'Thank you, Karrok,' Pell replied, bowing.

He stepped forwards and reached out for the orb, but a cold aura emanating from the ball stopped him from picking it up with his bare hands. Taking a moment to put on his gloves, he picked up the orb. Holding it as far from his body as he could, he walked swiftly across to Shadow and stuffed it deep into his saddlebag.

'You must go, and quickly,' the griffin said abruptly. 'We will keep your adversaries here until sunset, but beyond this we will not interfere. You do not have long. Do not waste the time we give you.'

Pell bowed again. 'Our thanks, Karrok, speaker for the griffins,' he said formally. 'The Oracle's message told us to seek your counsel. Is there anything else that we need to know?'

'It seems you have found some wisdom during your quest, human,' Karrok replied, inclining his head slightly to acknowledge Pell's bow. 'Seek the place where the shadows dwell. The answer to your questions awaits you there.'

Karrok's answer made no sense, but Pell realised he would get no more. He glanced up at the sky. The horsetails of cirrus he had noticed earlier were fast giving way to a sheet of high cloud. The bad weather was coming. So was dusk. They did not have long.

'Nolita?' he called. 'Can Firestorm heal Shadow's shoulder?'

'No,' she replied, her voice trembling. 'He says he can't, but he can use his fire to seal the wound.'

'*Do you want him to do it?*' Pell asked Shadow silently.

'*If he can stop me from losing any more blood, it will help me hold on to what strength I have left,*' she replied.

They had little choice. 'Do it,' Pell called back.

He looked one last time at Segun. The man's eyes were glaring at him with an icy fury that almost crackled.

'It isn't over, Pell,' Segun warned, his voice as chilling as his stare. 'You've got a long way to go and I'm going to be there every step of the way. You made the wrong choice and you will pay for it.'

Pell did not answer. He turned back to where Firestorm was positioning himself next to Shadow. Gritting his teeth, he braced himself for more pain.

# DRAGON ORB: FIRESTORM

Book 1 in the fantasy series.

## FOUR DRAGONRIDERS ON A MISSION TO SAVE THEIR WORLD

Nolita is terrified of dragons! Learning to fly her day dragon would be dangerous enough without irrational fears to contend with and a vicious dragonhunter on her tail.

With Elian, another novice rider, Nolita seeks the first of four orbs, whose combined power can save the leader of all dragonkind. Only Nolita, as a day dragonrider, can claim it. To do so, she must face her worst fears, and face them alone . . .

ISBN: 978-1-84738-068-5

# DRAGON ORB: LONGFANG

Book 3 in the fantasy series.

# FOUR DRAGONRIDERS ON A MISSION TO SAVE THEIR WORLD

Kira and her dusk dragon, Longfang, must find the
third orb to save the Oracle, leader of all dragonkind.
Following a path beset with dangers, and traps that maim and
kill, the four dragonriders must reach the twilight world of
the Castle of Shadows. Kira knows enough to be anxious.
What twisted sacrifice will this orb demand?

ISBN: 978-1-84738-070-8